YUKI-ONNA
AND OTHER STORIES

YUKI-ONNA
AND OTHER STORIES

LAFCADIO HEARN

Cover design: Peter Ridley
Cover illustration: Peter Gray

AD008446US

Printed in the UK

CONTENTS

INTRODUCTION

Lafcadio Hearn was born in 1850 in Levkás, Greece. His unusual name came from the island of his birth, though he did not spend long there, moving to Ireland when he was only two years old. His parents' marriage was not a happy one, and his mother returned to Greece in 1857, leaving Lafcadio in the care of his aunt, Sarah Holmes Brenane.

In 1869, Hearn decided to emigrate to the United States. He made his way to Cincinnati, Ohio, and he spent his first years there doing menial jobs to survive. His talent as a writer landed him a position as a journalist with the *Cincinnati Daily Enquirer* in 1872, and he distinguished himself through his sensationalist writing and exceptionally graphic accounts of local murders. In 1874, he married Alethea Foley, an African-American woman, but fell foul of Ohio's anti-miscegenation law and was fired from the *Enquirer*. The relationship with Foley was short lived, and the couple divorced in 1877.

Cincinnati no longer held the same appeal for Hearn, and so he moved to New Orleans in 1878, where he became fascinated by Creole culture and developed an interest in supernatural phenomena and the blurred boundaries between myth and reality which became enduring features of his life.

It was around this time that Hearn began writing fiction. Rarely more than a few paragraphs, they were a chance for him to demonstrate his unique gift to evoke an atmosphere that drew on his own experiences, but his stories found appeal in national magazines like *Harper's Weekly*. However, his wanderlust could not be restrained for long, and, in 1887, Hearn left to spend two years in Martinique as a correspondent.

Having returned to America, Hearn never felt truly at home and his life remained unsatisfying. He became increasingly disenchanted with Western society. In 1890, he made the most important decision of his life when he accepted a commission to visit Japan as a correspondent. It was a revelatory experience: Lafcadio fully embraced the traditional culture of his new home. He married a Japanese woman, Koizumi Setsu, and became an ardent supporter of traditional Japanese practices. Learning the language and adopting traditional dress, Hearn became more Japanese than the Japanese themselves.

He took it upon himself to preserve the legends and stories of ancient Japan from the onslaught of modernization and economic progress. A fervent admirer of Japanese culture, he aimed to share his fondness with a wider audience and recorded the folklore of the local population in the form of short stories written in English. These were some of his most powerful works, bringing to life the magic and mystery of the east.

Hearn's literary career reached its pinnacle in 1904 when he published *Kwaidan: Stories and Studies of Strange Things*, a fascinating collection of short stories featuring the legends, the spirits, and the enchantments of Japanese folklore.

This anthology includes a selection of his Japanese ghost stories, including such favorites as "Yuki-Onna," "Ingwa-Banashi," and "The Corpse-Rider." Across his writing the authenticity of his approach shines through, presenting a windo w into other worlds and offering an experience no other writer can deliver.

YUKI-ONNA

In a village of Musashi Province, there lived two woodcutters: Mosaku and Minokichi. At the time of which I am speaking, Mosaku was an old man; and Minokichi, his apprentice, was a lad of eighteen years. Every day they went together to a forest situated about five miles from their village. On the way to that forest there is a wide river to cross; and there is a ferry-boat. Several times a bridge was built where the ferry is; but the bridge was each time carried away by a flood. No common bridge can resist the current there when the river rises.

Mosaku and Minokichi were on their way home, one very cold evening, when a great snowstorm overtook them. They reached the ferry; and they found that the boatman had gone away, leaving his boat on the other side of the river. It was no day for swimming; and the woodcutters took shelter in the ferryman's hut—thinking themselves lucky to find any shelter at all. There was no brazier in the hut, nor any place in which to make a fire: it was only a two-mat[1] hut, with a single door, but no window. Mosaku and Minokichi fastened the door, and lay down to rest, with their straw rain-coats over them. At first they did not feel very cold; and they thought that the storm would soon be over.

The old man almost immediately fell asleep; but the boy, Minokichi, lay awake a long time, listening to the awful wind, and the continual slashing of the snow against the door. The river was roaring; and the hut swayed and creaked like a junk at sea. It was a terrible storm; and the air was every moment becoming colder; and Minokichi shivered under his rain-coat. But at last, in spite of the cold, he too fell asleep.

He was awakened by a showering of snow in his face. The door of the hut had been forced open; and, by the snow-light (*yuki-akari*), he saw a woman in the room—a woman all in

---

1   That is to say, with a floor-surface of about six feet square.

white. She was bending above Mosaku, and blowing her breath upon him;—and her breath was like a bright white smoke. Almost in the same moment she turned to Minokichi, and stooped over him. He tried to cry out, but found that he could not utter any sound. The white woman bent down over him, lower and lower, until her face almost touched him; and he saw that she was very beautiful—though her eyes made him afraid. For a little time she continued to look at him;—then she smiled, and she whispered:—"I intended to treat you like the other man. But I cannot help feeling some pity for you—because you are so young... You are a pretty boy, Minokichi; and I will not hurt you now. But, if you ever tell anybody—even your own mother—about what you have seen this night, I shall know it; and then I will kill you... Remember what I say!"

With these words, she turned from him, and passed through the doorway. Then he found himself able to move; and he sprang up, and looked out. But the woman was nowhere to be seen; and the snow was driving furiously into the hut. Minokichi closed the door, and secured it by fixing several billets of wood against it. He wondered if the wind had blown it open;—he thought that he might have been only dreaming, and might have mistaken the gleam of the snow-light in the doorway for the figure of a white woman: but he could not be sure. He called to Mosaku, and was frightened because the old man did not answer. He put out his hand in the dark, and touched Mosaku's face, and found that it was ice! Mosaku was stark and dead...

By dawn the storm was over; and when the ferryman returned to his station, a little after sunrise, he found Minokichi lying senseless beside the frozen body of Mosaku. Minokichi was promptly cared for, and soon came to himself; but he remained a long time ill from the effects of the cold of that terrible night. He had been greatly frightened also by the old man's death; but he said nothing about the vision of the woman in white. As soon as he got well again, he returned to his calling—going alone every morning to the forest, and coming back at nightfall with his bundles of wood, which his mother helped him to sell.

One evening, in the winter of the following year, as he was on his way home, he overtook a girl who happened to be traveling by the same road. She was a tall, slim girl, very good-looking; and she answered Minokichi's greeting in a voice as pleasant to the ear as the voice of a song-bird. Then he walked beside her; and they began to talk. The girl said that her name was O-Yuki;[2] that she had lately lost both of her parents; and that she was going to Yedo,[3] where she happened to have some poor relations, who might help her to find a situation as a servant. Minokichi soon felt charmed by this strange girl; and the more that he looked at her, the handsomer she appeared to be. He asked her whether she was yet betrothed; and she answered, laughingly, that she was free. Then, in her turn, she asked Minokichi whether he was married, or pledged to marry; and he told her that, although he had only a widowed mother to support, the question of an "honorable daughter-in-law" had not yet been considered, as he was very young... After these confidences, they walked on for a long while without speaking; but, as the proverb declares, *Ki ga areba, me mo kuchi hodo ni mono wo iu*: "When the wish is there, the eyes can say as much as the mouth." By the time they reached the village, they had become very much pleased with each other; and then Minokichi asked O-Yuki to rest awhile at his house. After some shy hesitation, she went there with him; and his mother made her welcome, and prepared a warm meal for her. O-Yuki behaved so nicely that Minokichi's mother took a sudden fancy to her, and persuaded her to delay her journey to Yedo. And the natural end of the matter was that Yuki never went to Yedo at all. She remained in the house, as an "honorable daughter-in-law."

---

2   This name, signifying "Snow," is not uncommon. On the subject of Japanese female names, see my paper in the volume entitled *Shadowings*.

3   Also spelled Edo, the former name of Tōkyō.

O-Yuki proved a very good daughter-in-law. When Minokichi's mother came to die—some five years later—her last words were words of affection and praise for the wife of her son. And O-Yuki bore Minokichi ten children, boys and girls—handsome children all of them, and very fair of skin.

The country-folk thought O-Yuki a wonderful person, by nature different from themselves. Most of the peasant-women age early; but O-Yuki, even after having become the mother of ten children, looked as young and fresh as on the day when she had first come to the village.

One night, after the children had gone to sleep, O-Yuki was sewing by the light of a paper lamp; and Minokichi, watching her, said:—

"To see you sewing there, with the light on your face, makes me think of a strange thing that happened when I was a lad of eighteen. I then saw somebody as beautiful and white as you are now—indeed, she was very like you."…

Without lifting her eyes from her work, O-Yuki responded:—

"Tell me about her… Where did you see her?"

Then Minokichi told her about the terrible night in the ferry-man's hut—and about the White Woman that had stooped above him, smiling and whispering—and about the silent death of old Mosaku. And he said:—

"Asleep or awake, that was the only time that I saw a being as beautiful as you. Of course, she was not a human being; and I was afraid of her—very much afraid—but she was so white!… Indeed, I have never been sure whether it was a dream that I saw, or the Woman of the Snow."…

O-Yuki flung down her sewing, and arose, and bowed above Minokichi where he sat, and shrieked into his face:—

"It was I—I—I! Yuki it was! And I told you then that I would kill you if you ever said one word about it!… But for those children asleep there, I would kill you this moment! And now you had better take very, very good care of them; for if ever they have reason to complain of you, I will treat you as you deserve!"…

Even as she screamed, her voice became thin, like a crying of wind;—then she melted into a bright white mist that spired to the roof-beams, and shuddered away through the smoke-hold... Never again was she seen.

THE STORY OF O-KAMÉ

O-Kamé, daughter of the rich Gonyemon of Nagoshi, in the province of Tosa, was very fond of her husband, Hachiye-mon. She was twenty-two, and Hachiyémon twenty-five. She was so fond of him that people imagined her to be jealous. But he never gave her the least cause for jealousy; and it is certain that no single unkind word was ever spoken between them.

Unfortunately the health of O-Kamé was feeble. Within less than two years after her marriage she was attacked by a disease, then prevalent in Tosa, and the best doctors were not able to cure her. Persons seized by this malady could not eat or drink; they remained constantly drowsy and languid, and troubled by strange fancies. And, in spite of constant care, O-Kamé grew weaker and weaker, day by day, until it became evident, even to herself, that she was going to die.

Then she called her husband, and said to him:

"I cannot tell you how good you have been to me during this miserable sickness of mine. Surely no one could have been more kind. But that only makes it all the harder for me to leave you now....Think! I am not yet even twenty-five, and I have the best husband in all this world, and yet I must die!... Oh, no, no! it is useless to talk to me about hope; the best Chinese doctors could do nothing for me. I did think to live a few months longer; but when I saw my face this morning in the mirror, I knew that I must die to-day, yes, this very day. And there is something that I want to beg you to do for me if you wish me to die quite happy."

"Only tell me what it is," Hachiyémon answered; "and if it be in my power to do, I shall be more than glad to do it."

"No, no you will not be glad to do it," she returned: "you are still so young! It is difficult very, very difficult even to ask you to do such a thing; yet the wish for it is like a fire burning in my breast. I must speak it before I die....My dear, you know that sooner or later, after I am dead, they will want you to take another wife. Will you promise me can you promise me not to marry again?..."

"Only that!" Hachiyémon exclaimed. "Why, if that be all that you wanted to ask for, your wish is very easily granted. With all my heart I promise you that no one shall ever take your place."

"*Aa! uréshiya!*" cried O-Kamé, half-rising from her couch; "Oh, how happy you have made me!"

And she fell back dead.

Now the health of Hachiyémon appeared to fail after the death of O-Kamé. At first the change in his aspect was attributed to natural grief, and the villagers only said, "How fond of her he must have been! "But, as the months went by, he grew paler and weaker, until at last he became so thin and wan that he looked more like a ghost than a man. Then people began to suspect that sorrow alone could not explain this sudden decline of a man so young. The doctors said that Hachiyémon was not suffering from any known form of disease: they could not account for his condition; but they suggested that it might have been caused by some very unusual trouble of mind. Hachiyémon's parents questioned him in vain; he had no cause for sorrow, he said, other than what they already knew. They counselled him to remarry; but he protested that nothing could ever induce him to break his promise to the dead.

Thereafter Hachiyémon continued to grow visibly weaker, day by day; and his family despaired of his life. But one day his mother, who felt sure that he had been concealing something from her, adjured him so earnestly to tell her the real cause of his decline, and wept so bitterly before him, that he was not able to resist her entreaties.

"Mother," he said, "it is very difficult to speak about this matter, either to you or to any one; and, perhaps, when I have told you everything, you will not be able to believe me. But the truth is that O-Kamé can find no rest in the other world, and that the Buddhist services repeated for her have been said in vain. Perhaps she will never be able to rest unless I go with her on the long black journey. For every night she returns, and lies down by my side. Every night, since the day of her funeral, she has come back. And sometimes I doubt if she be really dead; for she looks and acts just as when she lived, except that she talks to me only in whispers. And she always bids me tell no one that she comes. It may be that she wants me to die; and I should not care to live for my own sake only. But it is true, as you have said, that my body really belongs to my parents, and that I owe to them the first duty. So now, mother, I tell you the whole truth....Yes: every night she comes, just as I am about to sleep; and she remains until dawn. As soon as she hears the temple-bell, she goes away."

When the mother of Hachiyémon had heard these things, she was greatly alarmed; and, hastening at once to the parish-temple, she told the priest all that her son had confessed, and begged for ghostly help. The priest, who was a man of great age and experience, listened without surprise to the recital, and then said to her:

"It is not the first time that I have known such a thing to happen; and I think that I shall be able to save your son. But he is really in great danger. I have seen the shadow of death upon his face; and, if O-Kamé returns but once again, he will never behold another sunrise. Whatever can be done for him must be done quickly. Say nothing of the matter to your son; but assemble the members of both families as soon as possible, and tell them to come to the temple without delay. For your son's sake it will be necessary to open the grave of O-Kamé."

So the relatives assembled at the temple; and when the priest had obtained their consent to the opening of the sepulchre, he led the way to the cemetery. Then, under his direction, the tombstone of O-Kamé was shifted, the grave opened, and the coffin raised. And when the coffin-lid had been removed, all present were startled; for O-Kamé sat before them with a smile upon her face, seeming as comely as before the time of her sickness; and there was not any sign of death upon her. But when the priest told his assistants to lift the dead woman out of the coffin, the astonishment changed to fear; for the corpse was blood-warm to the touch, and still flexible as in life, notwithstanding the squatting posture in which it had remained so long.[4]

It was borne to the mortuary chapel; and there the priest, with a writing-brush, traced upon the brow and breast and limbs of the body the Sanscrit characters (Bonji) of certain holy talismanic words. And he performed a Segaki-service for the spirit of O-Kamé, before suffering her corpse to be restored to the ground.

She never again visited her husband; and Hachiyémon gradually recovered his health and strength. But whether he always kept his promise, the Japanese story-teller does not say.

---

4 The Japanese dead are placed in a sitting posture in the coffin, which is almost square in form.

OF A PROMISE KEPT

"I shall return in the early autumn," said Akana Soyëmon several hundred years ago,—when bidding good-bye to his brother by adoption, young Hasébé Samon. The time was spring; and the place was the village of Kato in the province of Harima. Akana was an Izumo samurai; and he wanted to visit his birthplace.

Hasébé said: —

"Your Izumo,—the Country of the Eight-Cloud Rising,[5]—is very distant. Perhaps it will therefore be difficult for you to promise to return here upon any particular day. But, if we were to know the exact day, we should feel happier. We could then prepare a feast of welcome; and we could watch at the gateway for your coming."

"Why, as for that," responded Akana, "I have been so much accustomed to travel that I can usually tell beforehand how long it will take me to reach a place; and I can safely promise you to be here upon a particular day. Suppose we say the day of the festival Chôyô?"

"That is the ninth day of the ninth month," said Hasébé;—"then the chrysanthemums will be in bloom, and we can go together to look at them. How pleasant!... So you promise to come back on the ninth day of the ninth month?"

"On the ninth day of the ninth month," repeated Akana, smiling farewell. Then he strode away from the village of Kato in the province of Harima;—and Hasébé Samon and the mother of Hasébé looked after him with tears in their eyes.

"Neither the Sun nor the Moon," says an old Japanese proverb, "ever halt upon their journey." Swiftly the months went by; and the autumn came,—the season of chrysanthemums. And early upon the morning of the ninth day of the ninth month Hasébé

5   One of the old poetical names for the Province of Izumo, or Unshū.

prepared to welcome his adopted brother. He made ready a feast
of good things, bought wine, decorated the guest-room, and filled
the vases of the alcove with chrysanthemums of two colors.
Then his mother, watching him, said:—"The province of Izumo,
my son, is more than one hundred *ri*[6] from this place; and the
journey thence over the mountains is difficult and weary; and
you cannot be sure that Akana will be able to come to-day. Would
it not be better, before you take all this trouble, to wait for his
coming?"

"Nay, mother!" Hasébé made answer—"Akana promised to be
here to-day: he could not break a promise! And if he were to
see us beginning to make preparation after his arrival, he would
know that we had doubted his word; and we should be put to
shame."

The day was beautiful, the sky without a cloud, and the air so
pure that the world seemed to be a thousand miles wider than
usual. In the morning many travellers passed through the village—
some of them samurai; and Hasébé, watching each as he came,
more than once imagined that he saw Akana approaching. But
the temple-bells sounded the hour of midday; and Akana did not
appear. Through the afternoon also Hasébé watched and waited
in vain. The sun set; and still there was no sign of Akana.
Nevertheless Hasébé remained at the gate, gazing down the road.
Later his mother went to him, and said:—"The mind of a man,
my son,—as our proverb declares—may change as quickly as
the sky of autumn. But your chrysanthemum-flowers will still be
fresh to-morrow. Better now to sleep; and in the morning you can
watch again for Akana, if you wish." "Rest well, mother," returned
Hasébé;—"but I still believe that he will come." Then the mother
went to her own room; and Hasébé lingered at the gate.

The night was pure as the day had been: all the sky throbbed
with stars; and the white River of Heaven shimmered with
unusual splendor. The village slept;—the silence was broken only

---

6   A *ri* is about equal to two and a half English miles.

by the noise of a little brook, and by the far-away barking of peasants' dogs. Hasébé still waited,—waited until he saw the thin moon sink behind the neighboring hills. Then at last he began to doubt and to fear. Just as he was about to re-enter the house, he perceived in the distance a tall man approaching,—very lightly and quickly; and in the next moment he recognized Akana.

"Oh!" cried Hasébé, springing to meet him—"I have been waiting for you from the morning until now!... So you really did keep your promise after all....But you must be tired, poor brother!—come in;—everything is ready for you." He guided Akana to the place of honor in the guest-room, and hastened to trim the lights, which were burning low. "Mother," continued Hasébé, "felt a little tired this evening, and she has already gone to bed; but I shall awaken her presently." Akana shook his head, and made a little gesture of disapproval. "As you will, brother," said Hasébé; and he set warm food and wine before the traveller. Akana did not touch the food or the wine, but remained motionless and silent for a short time. Then, speaking in a whisper,—as if fearful of awakening the mother, he said: —

"Now I must tell you how it happened that I came thus late. When I returned to Izumo I found that the people had almost forgotten the kindness of our former ruler, the good Lord Enya, and were seeking the favor of the usurper Tsunéhisa, who had possessed himself of the Tonda Castle. But I had to visit my cousin, Akana Tanji, though he had accepted service under Tsunéhisa, and was living, as a retainer, within the castle grounds. He persuaded me to present myself before Tsunéhisa: I yielded chiefly in order to observe the character of the new ruler, whose face I had never seen. He is a skilled soldier, and of great courage; but he is cunning and cruel. I found it necessary to let him know that I could never enter into his service. After I left his presence he ordered my cousin to detain me—to keep me confined within the house. I protested that I had promised to return to Harima upon the ninth day of the ninth month; but I was refused permission to go. I then hoped to escape from the castle at night; but

I was constantly watched; and until to-day I could find no way to fulfil my promise...."

"Until to-day!" exclaimed Hasébé in bewilderment;—"the castle is more than a hundred *ri* from here!"

"Yes," returned Akana; "and no living man can travel on foot a hundred *ri* in one day. But I felt that, if I did not keep my promise, you could not think well of me; and I remembered the ancient proverb, *Tama yoku ichi nichi ni sen ri wo yuku* ["The soul of a man can journey a thousand *ri* in a day"]. Fortunately I had been allowed to keep my sword;—thus only was I able to come to you....Be good to our mother."

With these words he stood up, and in the same instant disappeared.

Then Hasébé knew that Akana had killed himself in order to fulfil the promise.

At earliest dawn Hasébé Samon set out for the Castle Tonda, in the province of Izumo. Reaching Matsué, he there learned that, on the night of the ninth day of the ninth month, Akana Soyëmon had performed *harakiri* in the house of Akana Tanji, in the grounds of the castle. Then Hasébé went to the house of Akana Tanji, and reproached Akana Tanji for the treachery done, and slew him in the midst of his family, and escaped without hurt. And when the Lord Tsunéhisa had heard the story, he gave commands that Hasébé should not be pursued. For, although an unscrupulous and cruel man himself, the Lord Tsunéhisa could respect the love of truth in others, and could admire the friendship and the courage of Hasébé Samon.

OF A PROMISE BROKEN

I

" I am not afraid to die," said the dying wife;—"there is only one thing that troubles me now. I wish that I could know who will take my place in this house."

"My dear one," answered the sorrowing husband, "nobody shall ever take your place in my home. I will never, never marry again."

At the time that he said this he was speaking out of his heart; for he loved the woman whom he was about to lose.

"On the faith of a samurai?" she questioned, with a feeble smile.

"On the faith of a samurai," he responded,—stroking the pale thin face.

"Then, my dear one," she said, "you will let me be buried in the garden,—will you not?—near those plum-trees that we planted at the further end? I wanted long ago to ask this; but I thought, that if you were to marry again, you would not like to have my grave so near you. Now you have promised that no other woman shall take my place;—so I need not hesitate to speak of my wish....I want so much to be buried in the garden! I think that in the garden I should sometimes hear your voice, and that I should still be able to see the flowers in the spring."

"It shall be as you wish," he answered. "But do not now speak of burial: you are not so ill that we have lost all hope."

"I have," she returned;—"I shall die this morning....But you will bury me in the garden?"

"Yes," he said,—"under the shade of the plum-trees that we planted;—and you shall have a beautiful tomb there."

"And will you give me a little bell?"

"Bell—?"

"Yes: I want you to put a little bell in the coffin,—such a little bell as the Buddhist pilgrims carry. Shall I have it?"

"You shall have the little bell,—and anything else that you wish."

"I do not wish for anything else," she said.... "My dear one, you have been very good to me always. Now I can die happy."

Then she closed her eyes and died—as easily as a tired child falls asleep. She looked beautiful when she was dead; and there was a smile upon her face.

She was buried in the garden, under the shade of the trees that she loved; and a small bell was buried with her. Above the grave was erected a handsome monument, decorated with the family crest, and bearing the kaimyô:—*"Great Elder Sister, Luminous-Shadow-of-the-Plum-Flower-Chamber, dwelling in the Mansion of the Great Sea of Compassion."*

But, within a twelve-month after the death of his wife, the relatives and friends of the samurai began to insist that he should marry again. "You are still a young man," they said, "and an only son; and you have no children. It is the duty of a samurai to marry. If you die childless, who will there be to make the offerings and to remember the ancestors?"

By many such representations he was at last persuaded to marry again. The bride was only seventeen years old; and he found that he could love her dearly, notwithstanding the dumb reproach of the tomb in the garden.

II

Nothing took place to disturb the happiness of the young wife until the seventh day after the wedding,—when her husband was ordered to undertake certain duties requiring his presence at the castle by night. On the first evening that he was obliged to leave her alone, she felt uneasy in a way that she could not explain,—vaguely afraid without knowing why. When she went to bed she could not sleep. There was a strange oppression in the air,—an indefinable heaviness like that which sometimes precedes the coming of a storm.

About the Hour of the Ox she heard, outside in the night, the clanging of a bell,—a Buddhist pilgrim's bell;—and she wondered what pilgrim could be passing through the samurai quarter at such a time. Presently, after a pause, the bell sounded much nearer. Evidently the pilgrim was approaching the house;—but why approaching from the rear, where no road was?... Suddenly the dogs began to whine and howl in an unusual and horrible way;— and a fear came upon her like the fear of dreams....That ringing was certainly in the garden....She tried to get up to waken a servant. But she found that she could not rise,—could not move,— could not call....And nearer, and still more near, came the clang of the bell;—and oh! how the dogs howled!... Then, lightly as a shadow steals, there glided into the room a Woman,—though every door stood fast, and every screen unmoved,—a Woman robed in a grave-robe, and carrying a pilgrim's bell. Eyeless she came,— because she had long been dead;—and her loosened hair streamed down about her face;—and she looked without eyes through the tangle of it, and spoke without a tongue: —

"Not in this house,—not in this house shall you stay! Here I am mistress still. You shall go; and you shall tell to none the reason of your going. If you tell HIM, I will tear you into pieces!"

So speaking, the haunter vanished. The bride became senseless with fear. Until the dawn she so remained.

Nevertheless, in the cheery light of day, she doubted the reality of what she had seen and heard. The memory of the warning still weighed upon her so heavily that she did not dare to speak of the vision, either to her husband or to any one else; but she was almost able to persuade herself that she had only dreamed an ugly dream, which had made her ill.

On the following night, however, she could not doubt. Again, at the Hour of the Ox, the dogs began to howl and whine;—again the bell resounded,—approaching slowly from the garden;—again the listener vainly strove to rise and call;—again the dead came into the room, and hissed, —

"You shall go; and you shall tell to no one why you must go! If you even whisper it to HIM, I will tear you in pieces!"...

This time the haunter came close to the couch,—and bent and muttered and moved above it....

Next morning, when the samurai returned from the castle, his young wife prostrated herself before him in supplication: —

"I beseech you," she said, "to pardon my ingratitude and my great rudeness in thus addressing you: but I want to go home;—I want to go away at once."

"Are you not happy here?" he asked, in sincere surprise. "Has any one dared to be unkind to you during my absence?"

"It is not that—" she answered, sobbing. "Everybody here has been only too good to me....But I cannot continue to be your wife;—I must go away...."

"My dear," he exclaimed, in great astonishment, "it is very painful to know that you have had any cause for unhappiness in this house. But I cannot even imagine why you should want to go away—unless somebody has been very unkind to you.... Surely you do not mean that you wish for a divorce?"

She responded, trembling and weeping, —

"If you do not give me a divorce, I shall die!"

He remained for a little while silent,—vainly trying to think of some cause for this amazing declaration. Then, without betraying any emotion, he made answer: —

"To send you back now to your people, without any fault on your part, would seem a shameful act. If you will tell me a good reason for your wish,—any reason that will enable me to explain matters honorably,—I can write you a divorce. But unless you give me a reason, a good reason, I will not divorce you,—for the honor of our house must be kept above reproach."

And then she felt obliged to speak; and she told him everything,—adding, in an agony of terror, —

"Now that I have let you know, she will kill me!—she will kill me!..."

Although a brave man, and little inclined to believe in phantoms, the samurai was more than startled for the moment. But a simple and natural explanation of the matter soon presented itself to his mind.

"My dear," he said, "you are now very nervous; and I fear that someone has been telling you foolish stories. I cannot give you a divorce merely because you have had a bad dream in this house. But I am very sorry indeed that you should have been suffering in such a way during my absence. To-night, also, I must be at the castle; but you shall not be alone. I will order two of the retainers to keep watch in your room; and you will be able to sleep in peace. They are good men; and they will take all possible care of you."

Then he spoke to her so considerately and so affectionately that she became almost ashamed of her terrors, and resolved to remain in the house.

III

The two retainers left in charge of the young wife were big, brave, simple-hearted men,—experienced guardians of women and children. They told the bride pleasant stories to keep her cheerful. She talked with them a long time, laughed at their good-humored fun, and almost forgot her fears. When at last she lay down to sleep, the men-at-arms took their places in a corner of the room, behind a screen, and began a game of go,—speaking only in whispers, that she might not be disturbed. She slept like an infant.

But again at the Hour of the Ox she awoke with a moan of terror,—for she heard the bell!... It was already near, and was coming nearer. She started up; she screamed;—but in the room there was no stir,—only a silence as of death,—a silence growing,—a silence thickening. She rushed to the men-at-arms: they sat before their checker-table,—motionless,—each staring at the other with fixed eyes. She shrieked to them: she shook them: they remained as if frozen....

Afterwards they said that they had heard the bell,—heard also the cry of the bride,—even felt her try to shake them into wakefulness;—and that, nevertheless, they had not been able to move or speak. From the same moment they had ceased to hear or to see: a black sleep had seized upon them.

Entering his bridal-chamber at dawn, the samurai beheld, by the light of a dying lamp, the headless body of his young wife, lying in a pool of blood. Still squatting before their unfinished game, the two retainers slept. At their master's cry they sprang up, and stupidly stared at the horror on the floor....

The head was nowhere to be seen;—and the hideous wound showed that it had not been cut off, but torn off. A trail of blood led from the chamber to an angle of the outer gallery, where the storm-doors appeared to have been riven apart. The three men followed that trail into the garden,—over reaches of grass,—over spaces of sand,—along the bank of an iris-bordered pond,—under heavy shadowings of cedar and bamboo. And suddenly, at a turn, they found themselves face to face with a nightmare-thing that chippered like a bat: the figure of the long-buried woman, erect before her tomb,—in one hand clutching a bell, in the other the dripping head....For a moment the three stood numbed. Then one of the men-at-arms, uttering a Buddhist invocation, drew, and struck at the shape. Instantly it crumbled down upon the soil,—an empty scattering of grave-rags, bones, and hair;—and the bell rolled clanking out of the ruin. But the fleshless right hand, though parted from the wrist, still writhed;—and its fingers still gripped at the bleeding head,—and tore, and mangled,—as the claws of the yellow crab cling fast to a fallen fruit....

["That is a wicked story," I said to the friend who had related it. "The vengeance of the dead—if taken at all—should have been taken upon the man."

"Men think so," he made answer. "But that is not the way that a woman feels...."

He was right.]

THE LEGEND OF
YUREI-DAKI

Near the village of Kurosaka, in the province of Hōki, there is a waterfall called Yurei-Daki, or The Cascade of Ghosts. Why it is so called I do not know. Near the foot of the fall there is a small shintō shrine of the god of the locality, whom the people name Taki-Daimyōjin; and in front of the shrine is a little wooden money-box—saisen-bako—to receive the offerings of believers. And there is a story about that money-box.

One icy winter's evening, thirty-five years ago, the women and girls employed at a certain asa-toriba, or hemp-factory, in Kurosaka, gathered around the big brazier in the spinning-room after their day's work had been done. Then they amused themselves by telling ghost-stories. By the time that a dozen stories had been told, most of the gathering felt uncomfortable; and a girl cried out, just to heighten the pleasure of fear, "Only think of going this night, all by one's self, to the Yurei-Daki!" The suggestion provoked a general scream, followed by nervous bursts of laughter…. "I'll give all the hemp I spun to-day," mockingly said one of the party, "to the person who goes!" "So will I," exclaimed another. "And I," said a third. "All of us," affirmed a fourth…. Then from among the spinners stood up one Yasumoto O-Katsu, the wife of a carpenter;—she had her only son, a boy of two years old, snugly wrapped up and asleep upon her back. "Listen," said O-Katsu; "if you will all really agree to make over to me all the hemp spun to-day, I will go to the Yurei-Daki." Her proposal was received with cries of astonishment and of defiance. But after having been several times repeated, it was seriously taken. Each of the spinners in turn agreed to give up her share of the day's work to O-Katsu, providing that O-Katsu should go to the Yurei-Daki. "But how are we to know if she really goes there?" a sharp voice asked. "Why, let her bring back the money-box of the god," answered an old woman whom the spinners called Obaa-San, the Grandmother; "that will be proof enough"

"I'll bring it," cried O-Katsu. And out she darted into the street, with her sleeping boy upon her back.

The night was frosty, but clear. Down the empty street O-Katsu hurried; and she saw that all the house fronts were tightly closed, because of the piercing cold. Out of the village, and along the high road she ran—pichà-pichà—with the great silence of frozen rice-fields on either hand, and only the stars to light her. Half an hour she followed the open road; then she turned down a narrower way, winding under cliffs. Darker and rougher the path became as she proceeded; but she knew it well, and she soon heard the dull roar of the water. A few minutes more, and the way widened into a glen,—and the dull roar suddenly became a loud clamor,—and before her she saw, looming against a mass of blackness, the long glimmering of the fall. Dimly she perceived the shrine,—the money-box. She rushed forward,—put out her hand....

"Oi! O-Katsu-San!" suddenly called a warning voice about the crash of the water.

O-Katsu stood motionless,—stupefied by terror.

"Oi! O-Katsu-San!" again pealed the voice,—this time with more of menace in its tone.

But O-Katsu was really a bold woman. At once recovering from her stupefaction, she snatched up the money-box and ran. She neither heard nor saw anything more to alarm her until she reached the highroad, where she stopped a moment to take breath. Then she ran on steadily,—pichà-pichà,— till she got to Kurosaka, and thumped at the door of the asa-toriba.

How the women and the girls cried out as she entered, panting, with the money-box of the god in her hand! Breathlessly they heard her story; sympathetically they screeched when she told them of the Voice that had called her name, twice, out of the haunted water.... What a woman! Brave O-Katsu!—well had she earned the hemp!... "But your boy must be cold, O-Katsu!" cried the Obaa-San, "let us have him here by the fire!"

"He ought to hungry," exclaimed the mother; "I must give him his milk presently."...

"Poor O-Katsu!" said the Obaa-San, helping to remove the wraps in which the boy had been carried,—"why, you are all wet behind!" Then, with a husky scream, the helper vociferated, "Arà! it is blood!"

And out of the wrappings unfastened there fell to the floor a blood-soaked bundle of baby clothes that left exposed two very small brown feet, and two very small brown hands—nothing more.

The child's head had been torn off!...

INGWA-BANASHI

The daimyo's wife was dying, and knew that she was dying. She had not been able to leave her bed since the early autumn of the tenth Bunsei. It was now the fourth month of the twelfth Bunsei,—the year 1829 by Western counting; and the cherry-trees were blossoming. She thought of the cherry-trees in her garden, and of the gladness of spring. She thought of her children. She thought of her husband's various concubines—especially the Lady Yukiko, nineteen years old.

"My dear wife," said the daimyo, "you have suffered very much for three long years. We have done all that we could to get you well—watching beside you night and day, praying for you, and often fasting for your sake. But in spite of our loving care, and in spite of the skill of our best physicians, it would now seem that the end of your life is not far off. Probably we shall sorrow more than you will sorrow because of your having to leave what the Buddha so truly termed 'this burning-house of the world.' I shall order to be performed—no matter what the cost—every religious rite that can serve you in regard to your next rebirth; and all of us will pray without ceasing for you, that you may not have to wander in the Black Space, but nay quickly enter Paradise, and attain to Buddha-hood."

He spoke with the utmost tenderness, pressing her the while. Then, with eyelids closed, she answered him in a voice thin as the voice of in insect:—

"I am grateful—most grateful—for your kind words.... Yes, it is true, as you say, that I have been sick for three long years, and that I have been treated with all possible care and affection.... Why, indeed, should I turn away from the one true Path at the very moment of my death?... Perhaps to think of worldly matters at such a time is not right;—but I have one last request to make—only one.... Call here to me the Lady Yukiko;—you know that I love her like a sister. I want to speak to her about the affairs of this household."

Yukiko came at the summons of the lord, and, in obedience to a sign from him, knelt down beside the couch. The daimyo's wife opened her eyes, and looked at Yukiko, and spoke:—"Ah, here is Yukiko!... I am so pleased to see you, Yukiko!... Come a little closer—so that you can hear me well: I am not able to speak loud.... Yukiko, I am going to die. I hope that you will be faithful in all things to our dear lord;—for I want you to take my place when I am gone.... I hope that you will always be loved by him—yes, even a hundred times more than I have been—and that you will very soon be promoted to a higher rank, and become his honored wife.... And I beg of you always to cherish our dear lord: never allow another woman to rob you of his affection.... This is what I wanted to say to you, dear Yukiko.... Have you been able to understand?"

"Oh, my dear Lady," protested Yukiko, "do not, I entreat you, say such strange things to me! You well know that I am of poor and mean condition:—how could I ever dare to aspire to become the wife of our lord!"

"Nay, nay!" returned the wife, huskily—"this is not a time for words of ceremony: let us speak only the truth to each other. After my death, you will certainly be promoted to a higher place; and I now assure you again that I wish you to become the wife of our lord—yes, I wish this, Yukiko, even more than I wish to become a Buddha!... Ah, I had almost forgotten!—I want you to do something for me, Yukiko. You know that in the garden there is a *yaë-zakura*,[7] which was brought here, the year before last, from Mount Yoshino in Yamato. I have been told that it is now in full bloom;—and I wanted so much to see it in flower! In a little while I shall be dead;—I must see that tree before I die. Now I wish you to carry me into the garden—at once, Yukiko—so that I can see it.... Yes, upon your back, Yukiko;—take me upon your back...."

While thus asking, her voice had gradually become clear and strong—as if the intensity of the wish had given her new force:

---

7   *Yaë-zakura, yaë-no-sakura*, a variety of Japanese cherry-tree that bears double-blossoms.

then she suddenly burst into tears. Yukiko knelt motionless, not knowing what to do; but the lord nodded assent.

"It is her last wish in this world," he said. "She always loved cherry-flowers; and I know that she wanted very much to see that Yamato-tree in blossom. Come, my dear Yukiko, let her have her will."

As a nurse turns her back to a child, that the child may cling to it, Yukiko offered her shoulders to the wife, and said:—

"Lady, I am ready: please tell me how I best can help you."

"Why, this way!"—responded the dying woman, lifting herself with an almost superhuman effort by clinging to Yukiko's shoulders. But as she stood erect, she quickly slipped her thin hands down over the shoulders, under the robe, and clutched the breasts of the girl, and burst into a wicked laugh.

"I have my wish!" she cried—"I have my wish for the cherry-bloom,[8]—but not the cherry-bloom of the garden!... I could not die before I got my wish. Now I have it!—oh, what a delight!"

And with these words she fell forward upon the crouching girl, and died.

The attendants at once attempted to lift the body from Yukiko's shoulders, and to lay it upon the bed. But—strange to say!—this seemingly easy thing could not be done. The cold hands had attached themselves in some unaccountable way to the breasts of the girl—appeared to have grown into the quick flesh. Yukiko became senseless with fear and pain.

Physicians were called. They could not understand what had taken place. By no ordinary methods could the hands of the dead woman be unfastened from the body of her victim;—they so clung that any effort to remove them brought blood. This was not because the fingers held: it was because the flesh of the palms had united itself in some inexplicable manner to the flesh of the breasts!

---

8   In Japanese poetry and proverbial phraseology, the physical beauty of a woman is compared to the cherry-flower; while feminine moral beauty is compared to the plum-flower.

At that time the most skilful physician in Yedo was a foreigner,—a Dutch surgeon. It was decided to summon him. After a careful examination he said that he could not understand the case, and that for the immediate relief of Yukiko there was nothing to be done except to cut the hands from the corpse. He declared that it would be dangerous to attempt to detach them from the breasts. His advice was accepted; and the hands were amputated at the wrists. But they remained clinging to the breasts; and there they soon darkened and dried up—like the hands of a person long dead.

Yet this was only the beginning of the horror.

Withered and bloodless though they seemed, those hands were not dead. At intervals they would stir—stealthily, like great grey spiders. And nightly thereafter—beginning always at the Hour of the Ox,[9]—they would clutch and compress and torture. Only at the Hour of the Tiger the pain would cease.

Yukiko cut off her hair, and became a mendicant-nun—taking the religious name of Dassetsu. She had an *ibai* (mortuary tablet) made, bearing the kaimyō of her dead mistress—"Myō-Kō-In-Den Chizan-Ryō-Fu Daishi";—and this she carried about with her in all her wanderings; and every day before it she humbly besought the dead for pardon, and performed a Buddhist service in order that the jealous spirit might find rest. But the evil karma that had rendered such an affliction possible could not soon be exhausted. Every night at the Hour of the Ox, the hands never failed to torture her, during more than seventeen years—according to the testimony of those persons to whom she last told her story, when she stopped for one evening at the house of Noguchi Dengozayémon, in the village of Tanaka in the district of Kawachi in the province of Shimotsuké. This was in the third year of Kōkwa (1846). Thereafter nothing more was ever heard of her.

---

9   In ancient Japanese time, the Hour of the Ox was the special hour of ghosts. It began at 2 A.M., and lasted until 4 A.M.—for the old Japanese hour was double the length of the modern hour. The Hour of the Tiger began at 4 A.M.

THE CORPSE-RIDER

The body was cold as ice; the heart had long ceased to beat: yet there were no other signs of death. Nobody even spoke of burying the woman. She had died of grief and anger at having been divorced. It would have been useless to bury her—because the last undying wish of a dying person for vengeance can burst asunder any tomb and rift the heaviest graveyard stone. People who lived near the house in which she was lying fled from their homes. They knew that she was only *waiting for the return of the man who had divorced her*.

At the time of her death he was on a journey. When he came back and was told what had happened, terror seized him. "If I can find no help before dark," he thought to himself, "she will tear me to pieces." It was yet only the Hour of the Dragon;[10] but he knew that he had no time to lose.

He went at once to an *inyōshi*[11] and begged for succor. The *inyōshi* knew the story of the dead woman; and he had seen the body. He said to the supplicant:—"A very great danger threatens you. I will try to save you. But you must promise to do whatever I shall tell you to do. There is only one way by which you can be saved. It is a fearful way. But unless you find the courage to attempt it, she will tear you limb from limb. If you can be brave, come to me again in the evening before sunset." The man shuddered; but he promised to do whatever should be required of him.

At sunset the *inyōshi* went with him to the house where the body was lying. The *inyōshi* pushed open the sliding-doors, and told his client to enter. It was rapidly growing dark. "I dare not!"

---

10   *Tatsu no Koku*, or the Hour of the Dragon, by old Japanese time, began at about eight o'clock in the morning.

11   *Inyōshi*, a professor or master of the science of *in-yō*—the old Chinese nature-philosophy, based upon the theory of a male and a female principle pervading the universe.

gasped the man, quaking from head to foot;—"I dare not even look at her!"

"You will have to do much more than look at her," declared the *inyōshi*;—"and you promised to obey. Go in!" He forced the trembler into the house and led him to the side of the corpse.

The dead woman was lying on her face. "Now you must get astride upon her," said the *inyōshi*, "and sit firmly on her back, as if you were riding a horse.... Come!—you must do it!" The man shivered so that the *inyōshi* had to support him—shivered horribly; but he obeyed. "Now take her hair in your hands," commanded the *inyōshi*—"half in the right hand, half in the left.... So!... You must grip it like a bridle. Twist your hands in it—both hands—tightly. That is the way!... Listen to me! You must stay like that till morning. You will have reason to be afraid in the night—plenty of reason. But whatever may happen, never let go of her hair. If you let go—even for one second—she will tear you into gobbets!"

The *inyōshi* then whispered some mysterious words into the ear of the body, and said to its rider:—"Now, for my own sake, I must leave you alone with her.... Remain as you are!... Above all things, remember that you must not let go of her hair." And he went away—closing the doors behind him.

Hour after hour the man sat upon the corpse in black fear;—and the hush of the night deepened and deepened about him till he screamed to break it. Instantly the body sprang beneath him, as to cast him off; and the dead woman cried out loudly, "Oh, how heavy it is! Yet I shall bring that fellow here now!"

Then tall she rose, and leaped to the doors, and flung them open, and rushed into the night—always bearing the weight of the man. But he, shutting his eyes, kept his hands twisted in her long hair—tightly, tightly—though fearing with such a fear that he could not even moan. How far she went, he never knew. He saw nothing: he heard only the sound of her naked feet in the dark—*picha-picha, picha-picha*—and the hiss of her breathing as she ran.

At last she turned, and ran back into the house, and lay down upon the floor exactly as at first. Under the man she panted and moaned till the cocks began to crow. Thereafter she lay still.

But the man, with chattering teeth, sat upon her until the *inyōshi* came at sunrise. "So you did not let go of her hair!"— observed the *inyōshi*, greatly pleased. "That is well... Now you can stand up." He whispered again into the ear of the corpse, and then said to the man:—"You must have passed a fearful night; but nothing else could have saved you. Hereafter you may feel secure from her vengeance."

The conclusion of this story I do not think to be morally satisfying. It is not recorded that the corpse-rider became insane, or that his hair turned white: we are told only that "he worshiped the *inyōshi* with tears of gratitude." A note appended to the recital is equally disappointing. "It is reported," the Japanese author says, "that a grandchild of the man [*who rode the corpse*] still survives, and that a grandson of the *inyōshi* is at this very time living in a village called Otokunoi-mura [*probably pronounced Otonoi-mura*]."

This village-name does not appear in any Japanese directory of to-day. But the names of many towns and villages have been changed since the foregoing story was written.

A LEGEND OF
FUGEN-BOSATSU

There was once a very pious and learned priest, called Shōku Shōnin, who lived in the province of Harima. For many years he meditated daily upon the chapter of Fugen-Bosatsu [the Bodhisattva Samantabhadra] in the Sûtra of the Lotos of the Good Law; and he used to pray, every morning and evening, that he might at some time be permitted to behold Fugen-Bosatsu as a living presence, and in the form described in the holy text.[12]

One evening, while he was reciting the Sûtra, drowsiness overcame him; and he fell asleep leaning upon his *kyōsoku*.[13] Then he dreamed; and in his dream a voice told him that, in order to see Fugen-Bosatsu, he must go to the house of a certain courtesan, known as the "Yujō-no-Chōja,"[14] who lived in the town of Kanzaki. Immediately upon awakening he resolved to go to

---

12   The priest's desire was probably inspired by the promises recorded in the chapter entitled "The Encouragement of Samantabhadra" (see Kern's translation of the Saddharma Pundarîka in the *Sacred Books of the East*—pp 433-4):—"Then the Bodhisattva Mahâsattva Samantabhadra said to the Lord:...'When a preacher who applies himself to this Dharmaparyâya shall take a walk, then, O Lord, will I mount a white elephant with six tusks, and betake myself to the place where that preacher is walking, in order to protect this Dharmaparyâya. And when that preacher, applying himself to this Dharmaparyâya, forgets, be it but a single word or syllable, then will I mount the white elephant with six tusks, and show my face to that preacher, and repeat this entire Dharmaparyâya.'"—But these promises refer to "the end of time."

13   The *kyōsoku* is a kind of padded arm-rest, or arm-stool, upon which the priest leans one arm while reading. The use of such an arm-rest is not confined, however, to the Buddhist clergy.

14   A yujō, in old days, was a singing-girl as well as a courtesan. The term "Yujō-no-Chōja," in this case, would mean simply "the first (or best) of yujō."

Kanzaki;—and, making all possible haste, he reached the town by the evening of the next day.

When he entered the house of the *yujō*, he found many persons already there assembled—mostly young men of the capital, who had been attracted to Kanzaki by the fame of the woman's beauty. They were feasting and drinking; and the *yujō* was playing a small hand-drum (*tsuzumi*), which she used very skilfully, and singing a song. The song which she sang was an old Japanese song about a famous shrine in the town of Murozumi; and the words were these:—

Within the sacred water-tank[15] of Murozumi in Suwō,
Even though no wind be blowing,
The surface of the water is always rippling.

The sweetness of the voice filled everybody with surprise and delight. As the priest, who had taken a place apart, listened and wondered, the girl suddenly fixed her eyes upon him; and in the same instant he saw her form change into the form of Fugen-Bosatsu, emitting from her brow a beam of light that seemed to pierce beyond the limits of the universe, and riding a snow-white elephant with six tusks. And still she sang—but the song also was now transformed; and the words came thus to the ears of the priest:—

On the Vast Sea of Cessation,
Though the Winds of the Six Desires
and of the Five Corruptions never blow,
Yet the surface of that deep is always covered
With the billowings of Attainment to the Reality-in-Itself.

Dazzled by the divine ray, the priest closed his eyes: but through their lids he still distinctly saw the vision. When he opened them

---

15   *Mitarai. Mitarai* (or *mitarashi*) is the name especially given to the water-tanks, or water-fonts—of stone or bronze—placed before Shintō shrines in order that the worshipper may purify his lips and hands before making prayer. Buddhist tanks are not so named.

again, it was gone: he saw only the girl with her hand-drum, and heard only the song about the water of Murozumi. But he found that as often as he shut his eyes he could see Fugen-Bosatsu on the six-tusked elephant, and could hear the mystic Song of the Sea of Cessation. The other persons present saw only the *yujō*: they had not beheld the manifestation.

Then the singer suddenly disappeared from the banquet-room—none could say when or how. From that moment the revelry ceased; and gloom took the place of joy. After having waited and sought for the girl to no purpose, the company dispersed in great sorrow. Last of all, the priest departed, bewildered by the emotions of the evening. But scarcely had he passed beyond the gate, when the *yujō* appeared before him, and said:—"Friend, do not speak yet to any one of what you have seen this night." And with these words she vanished away—leaving the air filled with a delicious fragrance.

The monk by whom the foregoing legend was recorded, comments upon it thus:—The condition of a *yujō* is low and miserable, since she is condemned to serve the lusts of men. Who therefore could imagine that such a woman might be the *nirmanakaya*, or incarnation, of a Bodhisattva. But we must remember that the Buddhas and the Bodhisattvas may appear in this world in countless different forms; choosing, for the purpose of their divine compassion, even the most humble or contempt-ible shapes when such shapes can serve them to lead men into the true path, and to save them from the perils of illusion

THE STORY OF CHŪGORŌ

A long time ago there lived, in the Koishikawa quarter of Yedo, a hatamoto named Suzuki, whose yashiki was situated on the bank of the Yedogawa, not far from the bridge called Naka-no-hashi. And among the retainers of this Suzuki there was an ashigaru named Chūgorō. Chūgorō was a handsome lad, very amiable and clever, and much liked by his comrades.

For several years Chūgorō remained in the service of Suzuki, conducting himself so well that no fault was found with him. But at last the other ashigaru discovered that Chūgorō was in the habit of leaving the yashiki every night, by way of the garden, and staying out until a little before dawn. At first they said nothing to him about this strange behaviour; for his absences did not interfere with any regular duty, and were supposed to be caused by some love-affair. But after a time he began to look pale and weak; and his comrades, suspecting some serious folly, decided to interfere. Therefore, one evening, just as he was about to steal away from the house, an elderly retainer called him aside, and said:—

"Chūgorō, my lad, we know that you go out every night and stay away until early morning; and we have observed that you are looking unwell. We fear that you are keeping bad company, and injuring your health. And unless you can give a good reason for your conduct, we shall think that it is our duty to report this matter to the Chief Officer. In any case, since we are your comrades and friends, it is but right that we should know why you go out at night, contrary to the custom of this house."

Chūgorō appeared to be very much embarrassed and alarmed by those words. But after a short silence he passed into the garden, followed by his comrade. When the two found themselves well out of hearing of the rest, Chūgorō stopped, and said:—

"I will now tell you everything; but I must entreat you to keep my secret. If you repeat what I tell you, some great misfortune may befall me.

"It was in the early part of last spring—about five months ago—that I first began to go out at night, on account of a love-affair. One evening, when I was returning to the yashiki after a visit to my parents, I saw a woman standing by the riverside, not far from the main gateway. She was dressed like a person of high rank; and I thought it strange that a woman so finely dressed should be standing there alone at such an hour. But I did not think that I had any right to question her; and I was about to pass her by, without speaking, when she stepped forward and pulled me by the sleeve. Then I saw that she was very young and handsome. 'Will you not walk with me as far as the bridge?' she said; 'I have something to tell you.' Her voice was very soft and pleasant; and she smiled as she spoke; and her smile was hard to resist. So I walked with her toward the bridge; and on the way she told me that she had often seen me going in and out of the yashiki, and had taken a fancy to me. 'I wish to have you for my husband,' she said;—'if you can like me, we shall be able to make each other very happy.' I did not know how to answer her; but I thought her very charming. As we neared the bridge, she pulled my sleeve again, and led me down the bank to the very edge of the river. 'Come in with me,' she whispered, and pulled me toward the water. It is deep there, as you know; and I became all at once afraid of her, and tried to turn back. She smiled, and caught me by the wrist, and said, 'Oh, you must never be afraid with me!' And, somehow, at the touch of her hand, I became more helpless than a child. I felt like a person in a dream who tries to run, and cannot move hand or foot. Into the deep water she stepped, and drew me with her; and I neither saw nor heard nor felt anything more until I found myself walking beside her through what seemed to be a great palace, full of light. I was neither wet nor cold: everything around me was dry and warm and beautiful. I could not understand where I was, nor how I had come there. The woman led me by the hand: we passed through room after room,—through ever so many rooms, all empty, but very fine,—until we entered into a guest-room of a thousand mats. Before a great alcove, at the farther end, lights were burning, and cushions laid as for feast; but I saw no guests. She led me to the place of honour, by the alcove, and seated herself in front of me, and said: 'This is my home: do you think that you could be happy with me here?' As she asked the question she smiled; and I thought that her smile was more beautiful than anything else in the world; and out of my heart I answered, 'Yes....' In the same moment I remembered the story of Urashima; and I imagined that she might be the daughter of a god; but I feared to ask her any questions.... Presently maid-servants came in, bearing rice-wine and many dishes, which they set before us. Then she who sat before me said: 'To-night shall be our bridal night, because you like me; and this is our wedding-feast.' We pledged ourselves to each other for the time of seven existences; and after the banquet we were conducted to a bridal chamber, which had been prepared for us.

"It was yet early in the morning when she awoke me, and said: 'My dear one, you are now indeed my husband. But for reasons which I cannot tell you, and which you must not ask, it is necessary that our marriage remain secret. To keep you here until daybreak would cost both of us our lives. Therefore do not, I beg of you, feel displeased because I must now send you back to the house of your lord. You can come to me to-night again, and every night here-after, at the same hour that we first met. Wait always for me by the bridge; and you will not have to wait long. But remember, above all things, that our marriage must be a secret, and that, if you talk about it, we shall probably be separated forever.'

"I promised to obey her in all things,—remembering the fate of Urashima,—and she conducted me through many rooms, all empty and beautiful, to the entrance. There she again took me by the wrist, and everything suddenly became dark, and I knew nothing more until I found myself standing alone on the river bank, close to the Naka-no-hashi. When I got back to the yashiki, the temple bells had not yet begun to ring.

"In the evening I went again to the bridge, at the hour she had named, and I found her waiting for me. She took me with her, as before, into the deep water, and into the wonderful place where we had passed our bridal night. And every night, since then, I have met and parted from her in the same way. To-night she will certainly be waiting for me, and I would rather die than disappoint her: therefore I must go.... But let me again entreat you, my friend, never to speak to any one about what I have told you."

The elder ashigaru was surprised and alarmed by this story. He felt that Chūgorō had told him the truth; and the truth suggested unpleasant possibilities. Probably the whole experience was an illusion, and an illusion produced by some evil power for a malevolent end. Nevertheless, if really bewitched, the lad was rather to be pitied than blamed; and any forcible interference would be likely to result in mischief. So the ashigaru answered kindly:—

"I shall never speak of what you have told me—never, at least, while you remain alive and well. Go and meet the woman; but— beware of her! I fear that you are being deceived by some wicked spirit."

Chūgorō only smiled at the old man's warning, and hastened away. Several hours later he reentered the yashiki, with a strangely dejected look. "Did you meet her?" whispered his comrade. "No," replied Chūgorō; "she was not there. For the first time, she was not there. I think that she will never meet me again. I did wrong to tell you;—I was very foolish to break my promise...." The other vainly tried to console him. Chūgorō lay down, and spoke no word more. He was trembling from head to foot, as if he had caught a chill.

When the temple bells announced the hour of dawn, Chūgorō tried to get up, and fell back senseless. He was evidently sick,— deathly sick. A Chinese physician was summoned.

"Why, the man has no blood!" exclaimed the doctor, after a careful examination;—"there is nothing but water in his veins! It will be very difficult to save him.... What maleficence is this?"

Everything was done that could be done to save Chūgorō's life—but in vain. He died as the sun went down. Then his comrade related the whole story.

"Ah! I might have suspected as much!" exclaimed the doctor.... "No power could have saved him. He was not the first whom she destroyed."

"Who is she?—or what is she?" the ashigaru asked,—"a Fox-Woman?"

"No; she has been haunting this river from ancient time. She loves the blood of the young...."

"A Serpent-Woman?—A Dragon-Woman?"

"No, no! If you were to see her under that bridge by daylight, she would appear to you a very loathsome creature."

"But what kind of a creature?"

"Simply a Frog,—a great and ugly Frog!"

JIKININKI

Once, when Muso Kokushi, a priest of the Zen sect, was journeying alone through the province of Mino, he lost his way in a mountain-district where there was nobody to direct him. For a long time he wandered about helplessly; and he was beginning to despair of finding shelter for the night, when he perceived, on the top of a hill lighted by the last rays of the sun, one of those little hermitages, called *anjitsu*, which are built for solitary priests. It seemed to be in ruinous condition; but he hastened to it eagerly, and found that it was inhabited by an aged priest, from whom he begged the favor of a night's lodging. This the old man harshly refused; but he directed Muso to a certain hamlet, in the valley adjoining where lodging and food could be obtained.

Muso found his way to the hamlet, which consisted of less than a dozen farm-cottages; and he was kindly received at the dwelling of the headman. Forty or fifty persons were assembled in the principal apartment, at the moment of Muso's arrival; but he was shown into a small separate room, where he was promptly supplied with food and bedding. Being very tired, he lay down to rest at an early hour; but a little before midnight he was roused from sleep by a sound of loud weeping in the next apartment. Presently the sliding-screens were gently pushed apart; and a young man, carrying a lighted lantern, entered the room, respectfully saluted him, and said:—

"Reverend Sir, it is my painful duty to tell you that I am now the responsible head of this house. Yesterday I was only the eldest son. But when you came here, tired as you were, we did not wish that you should feel embarrassed in any way: therefore we did not tell you that father had died only a few hours before. The people whom you saw in the next room are the inhabitants of this village: they all assembled here to pay their last respects to the dead; and now they are going to another village, about three miles off—for by our custom, no one of us may remain in this village during the night after a death has taken place. We make the proper offerings and prayers;—then we go away, leaving the corpse alone. Strange things always happen in the house where a corpse has thus been left: so we think that it will be better for you to come away with us. We can find you good lodging in the other village. But perhaps, as you are a priest, you have no fear of demons or evil spirits; and, if you are not afraid of being left alone with the body, you will be very welcome to the use of this poor house. However, I must tell you that nobody, except a priest, would dare to remain here tonight."

Muso made answer:—

"For your kind intention and your generous hospitality, I am deeply grateful. But I am sorry that you did not tell me of your father's death when I came;—for, though I was a little tired, I certainly was not so tired that I should have found difficulty in doing my duty as a priest. Had you told me, I could have performed the service before your departure. As it is, I shall perform the service after you have gone away; and I shall stay by the body until morning. I do not know what you mean by your words about the danger of staying here alone; but I am not afraid of ghosts or demons: therefore please to feel no anxiety on my account."

The young man appeared to be rejoiced by these assurances, and expressed his gratitude in fitting words. Then the other members of the family, and the folk assembled in the adjoining room, having been told of the priest's kind promises, came to thank him—after which the master of the house said:—

"Now, reverend Sir, much as we regret to leave you alone, we must bid you farewell. By the rule of our village, none of us can stay here after midnight. We beg, kind Sir, that you will take every care of your honorable body, while we are unable to attend upon you. And if you happen to hear or see anything strange during our absence, please tell us of the matter when we return in the morning."

All then left the house, except the priest, who went to the room where the dead body was lying. The usual offerings had been set before the corpse; and a small Buddhist lamp—*tomyo*—was burning. The priest recited the service, and performed the funeral ceremonies—after which he entered into meditation. So meditating he remained through several silent hours; and there was no sound in the deserted village. But, when the hush of the night was at its deepest, there noiselessly entered a Shape, vague and vast; and in the same moment Muso found himself without power to move or speak. He saw that Shape lift the corpse, as with hands, devour it, more quickly than a cat devours a rat—beginning at the head, and eating everything: the hair and the bones and even the shroud. And the monstrous Thing, having thus consumed the body, turned to the offerings, and ate them also. Then it went away, as mysteriously as it had come.

When the villagers returned next morning, they found the priest awaiting them at the door of the headman's dwelling. All in turn saluted him; and when they had entered, and looked about the room, no one expressed any surprise at the disappearance of the dead body and the offerings. But the master of the house said to Muso:—

"Reverend Sir, you have probably seen unpleasant things during the night: all of us were anxious about you. But now we are very happy to find you alive and unharmed. Gladly we would have stayed with you, if it had been possible. But the law of our village, as I told you last evening, obliges us to quit our houses after a death has taken place, and to leave the corpse alone. Whenever this law has been broken, heretofore, some great misfortune has followed. Whenever it is obeyed, we find that the corpse and the offerings disappear during our absence. Perhaps you have seen the cause."

Then Muso told of the dim and awful Shape that had entered the death-chamber to devour the body and the offerings. No person seemed to be surprised by his narration; and the master of the house observed:—

"What you have told us, reverend Sir, agrees with what has been said about this matter from ancient time."

Muso then inquired:—

"Does not the priest on the hill sometimes perform the funeral service for your dead?"

"What priest?" the young man asked.

"The priest who yesterday evening directed me to this village," answered Muso. "I called at his *anjitsu* on the hill yonder. He refused me lodging, but told me the way here."

The listeners looked at each other, as in astonishment; and, after a moment of silence, the master of the house said:—

"Reverend Sir, there is no priest and there is no *anjitsu* on the hill. For the time of many generations there has not been any resident-priest in this neighborhood."

Muso said nothing more on the subject; for it was evident that his kind hosts supposed him to have been deluded by some goblin. But after having bidden them farewell, and obtained all necessary information as to his road, he determined to look again for the hermitage on the hill, and so to ascertain whether he had really been deceived. He found the *anjitsu* without any difficulty; and, this time, its aged occupant invited him to enter. When he had done so, the hermit humbly bowed down before him, exclaiming:—"Ah! I am ashamed!—I am very much ashamed!—I am exceedingly ashamed!"

"You need not be ashamed for having refused me shelter," said Muso. "You directed me to the village yonder, where I was very kindly treated; and I thank you for that favor."

"I can give no man shelter," the recluse made answer;—"and it is not for the refusal that I am ashamed. I am ashamed only that you should have seen me in my real shape—for it was I who devoured the corpse and the offerings last night before your eyes... Know, reverend Sir, that I am a *jikininki*,[16]—an eater of human flesh. Have pity upon me, and suffer me to confess the secret fault by which I became reduced to this condition.

"A long, long time ago, I was a priest in this desolate region.

There was no other priest for many leagues around. So, in that time, the bodies of the mountain-folk who died used to be brought here—sometimes from great distances—in order that I might repeat over them the holy service. But I repeated the service and performed the rites only as a matter of business;—I thought only of the food and the clothes that my sacred profession enabled me to gain. And because of this selfish impiety I was reborn, immediately after my death, into the state of a *jikininki.* Since then I have been obliged to feed upon the corpses of the people who die in this district: every one of them I must devour in the way that you saw last night... Now, reverend Sir, let me beseech you to perform a *Segaki*-service[17] for me: help me by your prayers, I entreat you, so that I may be soon able to escape from this horrible state of existence..."

No sooner had the hermit uttered this petition than he disappeared; and the hermitage also disappeared at the same instant. And Muso Kokushi found himself kneeling alone in the high grass, beside an ancient and moss-grown tomb of the form called *go-rin-ishi,*[18] which seemed to be the tomb of a priest.

---

16   Literally, a man-eating goblin. The Japanese narrator gives also the Sanscrit term, "Rakshasa;" but this word is quite as vague as *jikininki,* since there are many kinds of Rakshasas. Apparently the word *jikininki* signifies here one of the *Baramon-Rasetsu-Gaki*—forming the twenty-sixth class of pretas enumerated in the old Buddhist books.

17   A *Segaki*-service is a special Buddhist service performed on behalf of beings supposed to have entered into the condition of *gaki* (pretas), or hungry spirits. For a brief account of such a service, see my Japanese Miscellany.

18   Literally, "five-circle [or five-zone] stone." A funeral monument consisting of five parts superimposed—each of a different form—symbolizing the five mystic elements: Ether, Air, Fire, Water, Earth.

THE STORY OF AOYAGI

In the era of Bummei [1469–86] there was a young samurai called Tomotada in the service of Hatakeyama Yoshimune, the Lord of Noto. Tomotada was a native of Echizen; but at an early age he had been taken, as page, into the palace of the daimyo of Noto, and had been educated, under the supervision of that prince, for the profession of arms. As he grew up, he proved himself both a good scholar and a good soldier, and continued to enjoy the favor of his prince. Being gifted with an amiable character, a winning address, and a very handsome person, he was admired and much liked by his samurai-comrades.

When Tomotada was about twenty years old, he was sent upon a private mission to Hosokawa Masamoto, the great daimyo of Kyoto, a kinsman of Hatakeyama Yoshimune. Having been ordered to journey through Echizen, the youth requested and obtained permission to pay a visit, on the way, to his widowed mother.

It was the coldest period of the year when he started; and, though mounted upon a powerful horse, he found himself obliged to proceed slowly. The road which he followed passed through a mountain-district where the settlements were few and far between; and on the second day of his journey, after a weary ride of hours, he was dismayed to find that he could not reach his intended halting-place until late in the night. He had reason to be anxious;—for a heavy snowstorm came on, with an intensely cold wind; and the horse showed signs of exhaustion. But in that trying moment, Tomotada unexpectedly perceived the thatched room of a cottage on the summit of a near hill, where willow-trees were growing. With difficulty he urged his tired animal to the dwelling; and he loudly knocked upon the storm-doors, which had been closed against the wind. An old woman opened them, and cried out compassionately at the sight of the handsome stranger: "Ah, how pitiful!—a young gentleman traveling alone in such weather!... Deign, young master, to enter."

Tomotada dismounted, and after leading his horse to a shed in the rear, entered the cottage, where he saw an old man and a girl warming themselves by a fire of bamboo splints. They respectfully invited him to approach the fire; and the old folks then proceeded to warm some rice-wine, and to prepare food for the traveler, whom they ventured to question in regard to his journey. Meanwhile the young girl disappeared behind a screen. Tomotada had observed, with astonishment, that she was extremely beautiful—though her attire was of the most wretched kind, and her long, loose hair in disorder. He wondered that so handsome a girl should be living in such a miserable and lonesome place.

The old man said to him:—

"Honored Sir, the next village is far; and the snow is falling thickly. The wind is piercing; and the road is very bad. Therefore, to proceed further this night would probably be dangerous. Although this hovel is unworthy of your presence, and although we have not any comfort to offer, perhaps it were safer to remain to-night under this miserable roof... We would take good care of your horse."

Tomotada accepted this humble proposal—secretly glad of the chance thus afforded him to see more of the young girl. Presently a coarse but ample meal was set before him; and the girl came from behind the screen, to serve the wine. She was now reclad, in a rough but clean robe of homespun; and her long, loose hair had been neatly combed and smoothed. As she bent forward to fill his cup, Tomotada was amazed to perceive that she was incomparably more beautiful than any woman whom he had ever before seen; and there was a grace about her every motion that astonished him. But the elders began to apologize for her, saying: "Sir, our daughter, Aoyagi,[19] has been

---

19   The name signifies "Green Willow;"—though rarely met with, it is still in use.

brought up here in the mountains, almost alone; and she knows nothing of gentle service. We pray that you will pardon her stupidity and her ignorance." Tomotada protested that he deemed himself lucky to be waited upon by so comely a maiden. He could not turn his eyes away from her—though he saw that his admiring gaze made her blush;—and he left the wine and food untasted before him. The mother said: "Kind Sir, we very much hope that you will try to eat and to drink a little—though our peasant-fare is of the worst—as you must have been chilled by that piercing wind." Then, to please the old folks, Tomotada ate and drank as he could; but the charm of the blushing girl still grew upon him. He talked with her, and found that her speech was sweet as her face. Brought up in the mountains as she might have been;—but, in that case, her parents must at some time been persons of high degree; for she spoke and moved like a damsel of rank. Suddenly he addressed her with a poem—which was also a question—inspired by the delight in his heart:—

"Tadzunetsuru,
Hana ka tote koso,
Hi wo kurase,
Akenu ni otoru
Akane sasuran?"[20]

Without a moment's hesitation, she answered him in these verses:—

20   The poem may be read in two ways; several of the phrases having a double meaning. But the art of its construction would need considerable space to explain, and could scarcely interest the Western reader. The meaning which Tomotada desired to convey might be thus expressed:—"While journeying to visit my mother, I met with a being lovely as a flower; and for the sake of that lovely person, I am passing the day here... Fair one, wherefore that dawn-like blush before the hour of dawn?—can it mean that you love me?"

"*Izuru hi no
Honomeku iro wo
Waga sode ni
Tsutsumaba asu mo
Kimiya tomaran.*"[21]

Then Tomotada knew that she accepted his admiration; and he was scarcely less surprised by the art with which she had uttered her feelings in verse, than delighted by the assurance which the verses conveyed. He was now certain that in all this world he could not hope to meet, much less to win, a girl more beautiful and witty than this rustic maid before him; and a voice in his heart seemed to cry out urgently, "Take the luck that the gods have put in your way!" In short he was bewitched—bewitched to such a degree that, without further preliminary, he asked the old people to give him their daughter in marriage—telling them, at the same time, his name and lineage, and his rank in the train of the Lord of Noto.

They bowed down before him, with many exclamations of grateful astonishment. But, after some moments of apparent hesitation, the father replied:—

"Honored master, you are a person of high position, and likely to rise to still higher things. Too great is the favor that you deign to offer us;—indeed, the depth of our gratitude therefore is not to be spoken or measured. But this girl of ours, being a stupid country-girl of vulgar birth, with no training or teaching of any sort, it would be improper to let her become the wife of a noble samurai. Even to speak of such a matter is not right... But, since you find the girl to your liking, and have condescended to pardon her peasant-manners and to overlook her great rudeness, we do gladly present her to you, for a humble handmaid. Deign, therefore, to act hereafter in her regard according to your august pleasure."

---

21   Another reading is possible; but this one gives the signification of the answer intended.

Ere morning the storm had passed; and day broke through a cloudless east. Even if the sleeve of Aoyagi hid from her lover's eyes the rose-blush of that dawn, he could no longer tarry. But neither could he resign himself to part with the girl; and, when everything had been prepared for his journey, he thus addressed her parents:—

"Though it may seem thankless to ask for more than I have already received, I must again beg you to give me your daughter for a wife. It would be difficult for me to separate from her now; and as she is willing to accompany me, if you permit, I can take her with me as she is. If you will give her to me, I shall ever cherish you as parents... And, in the meantime, please to accept this poor acknowledgment of your kindest hospitality."

So saying, he placed before his humble host a purse of gold *ryō*. But the old man, after many prostrations, gently pushed back the gift, and said:—

"Kind master, the gold would be of no use to us; and you will probably have need of it during your long, cold journey. Here we buy nothing; and we could not spend so much money upon ourselves, even if we wished... As for the girl, we have already bestowed her as a free gift;—she belongs to you: therefore it is not necessary to ask our leave to take her away. Already she has told us that she hopes to accompany you, and to remain your servant for as long as you may be willing to endure her presence. We are only too happy to know that you deign to accept her; and we pray that you will not trouble yourself on our account. In this place we could not provide her with proper clothing—much less with a dowry. Moreover, being old, we should in any event have to separate from her before long. Therefore it is very fortunate that you should be willing to take her with you now."

It was in vain that Tomotada tried to persuade the old people to accept a present: he found that they cared nothing for money. But he saw that they were really anxious to trust their daughter's fate to his hands; and he therefore decided to take her with him.

So he placed her upon his horse, and bade the old folks farewell for the time being, with many sincere expressions of gratitude.

"Honored Sir," the father made answer, "it is we, and not you, who have reason for gratitude. We are sure that you will be kind to our girl; and we have no fears for her sake."...

[Here, in the Japanese original, there is a queer break in the natural course of the narration, which therefrom remains curiously inconsistent. Nothing further is said about the mother of Tomotada, or about the parents of Aoyagi, or about the daimyo of Noto. Evidently the writer wearied of his work at this point, and hurried the story, very carelessly, to its startling end. I am not able to supply his omissions, or to repair his faults of construction; but I must venture to put in a few explanatory details, without which the rest of the tale would not hold together... It appears that Tomotada rashly took Aoyagi with him to Kyoto, and so got into trouble; but we are not informed as to where the couple lived afterwards.]

...Now a samurai was not allowed to marry without the consent of his lord; and Tomotada could not expect to obtain this sanction before his mission had been accomplished. He had reason, under such circumstances, to fear that the beauty of Aoyagi might attract dangerous attention, and that means might be devised of taking her away from him. In Kyoto he therefore tried to keep her hidden from curious eyes. But a retainer of Lord Hosokawa one day caught sight of Aoyagi, discovered her relation to Tomotada, and reported the matter to the daimyo. Thereupon the daimyo—a young prince, and fond of pretty faces—gave orders that the girl should be brought to the palace; and she was taken thither at once, without ceremony.

Tomotada sorrowed unspeakably; but he knew himself powerless. He was only an humble messenger in the service of a far-off daimyo; and for the time being he was at the mercy of a much more powerful daimyo, whose wishes were not to be questioned. Moreover Tomotada knew that he had acted foolishly—that he had brought about his own misfortune, by entering into a clandestine relation which the code of the military class condemned. There was now but one hope for him—a desperate hope: that Aoyagi might be able and willing to escape and to flee with him. After long reflection, he resolved to try to send her a letter. The attempt would be dangerous, of course: any writing sent to her might find its way to the hands of the daimyo; and to send a love-letter to any inmate of the palace was an unpardonable offense. But he resolved to dare the risk; and, in the form of a Chinese poem, he composed a letter which he endeavored to have conveyed to her. The poem was written with only twenty-eight characters. But with those twenty-eight characters he was about to express all the depth of his passion, and to suggest all the pain of his loss:—[22]

> *Koshi o-son gojin wo ou;*
> *Ryokuju namida wo tarete rakin wo hitataru;*
> *Komon hitotabi irite fukaki koto umi no gotoshi;*
> *Kore yori shoro kore rojin.*

> *[Closely, closely the youthful prince now follows after the*
>   *gem-bright maid;—*
> *The tears of the fair one, falling, have moistened all her*
>   *robes.*
> *But the august lord, having once become enamored of*
>   *her—the depth of his longing is like the depth of the sea.*
> *Therefore it is only I that am left forlorn—only I that am*
>   *left to wander along.]*

On the evening of the day after this poem had been sent, Tomotada was summoned to appear before the Lord Hosokawa. The youth at once suspected that his confidence had been betrayed; and he could not hope, if his letter had been seen by the daimyo, to escape the severest penalty. "Now he will order

22   So the Japanese story-teller would have us believe—although the verses seem commonplace in translation. I have tried to give only their general meaning: an effective literal translation would require some scholarship.

my death," thought Tomotada;—"but I do not care to live unless Aoyagi be restored to me. Besides, if the death-sentence be passed, I can at least try to kill Hosokawa." He slipped his swords into his girdle, and hastened to the palace.

On entering the presence-room he saw the Lord Hosokawa seated upon the dais, surrounded by samurai of high rank, in caps and robes of ceremony. All were silent as statues; and while Tomotada advanced to make obeisance, the hush seemed to his sinister and heavy, like the stillness before a storm. But Hosokawa suddenly descended from the dais, and, while taking the youth by the arm, began to repeat the words of the poem:—"*Koshi o-son gojin wo ou.*"... And Tomotada, looking up, saw kindly tears in the prince's eyes.

Then said Hosokawa:—

"Because you love each other so much, I have taken it upon myself to authorize your marriage, in lieu of my kinsman, the Lord of Noto; and your wedding shall now be celebrated before me. The guests are assembled;—the gifts are ready."

At a signal from the lord, the sliding-screens concealing a further apartment were pushed open; and Tomotada saw there many dignitaries of the court, assembled for the ceremony, and Aoyagi awaiting him in bride's apparel... Thus was she given back to him;—and the wedding was joyous and splendid;—and precious gifts were made to the young couple by the prince, and by the members of his household.

For five happy years, after that wedding, Tomotada and Aoyagi dwelt together. But one morning Aoyagi, while talking with her husband about some household matter, suddenly uttered a great cry of pain, and then became very white and still. After a few moments she said, in a feeble voice: "Pardon me for thus rudely crying out—but the pain was so sudden!... My dear husband, our union must have been brought about through some Karma-relation in a former state of existence; and that happy relation, I think, will bring us again together in more than one life to come. But for this present existence of ours, the relation is now ended;—

we are about to be separated. Repeat for me, I beseech you, the *Nembutsu*-prayer—because I am dying."

"Oh! What strange wild fancies!" cried the startled husband— "You are only a little unwell, my dear one!... lie down for a while, and rest; and the sickness will pass."...

"No, no!" she responded—"I am dying!—I do not imagine it;—I know!... And it were needless now, my dear husband, to hide the truth from you any longer:—I am not a human being. The soul of a tree is my soul;—the heart of a tree is my heart;— the sap of the willow is my life. And someone, at this cruel moment, is cutting down my tree;—that is why I must die!... Even to weep were now beyond my strength!—quickly, quickly repeat the *Nembutsu* for me... quickly!... Ah!..."

With another cry of pain she turned aside her beautiful head, and tried to hide her face behind her sleeve. But almost in the same moment her whole form appeared to collapse in the strangest way, and to sink down, down, down—level with the floor. Tomotada had sprung to support her;—but there was nothing to support! There lay on the matting only the empty robes of the fair creature and the ornaments that she had worn in her hair: the body had ceased to exist...

Tomotada shaved his head, took the Buddhist vows, and became an itinerant priest. He traveled through all the provinces of the empire; and, at holy places which he visited, he offered up prayers for the soul of Aoyagi. Reaching Echizen, in the course of his pilgrimage, he sought the home of the parents of his beloved. But when he arrived at the lonely place among the hills, where their dwelling had been, he found that the cottage had disappeared. There was nothing to mark even the spot where it had stood, except the stumps of three willows—two old trees and one young tree—that had been cut down long before his arrival.

Beside the stumps of those willow-trees he erected a memorial tomb, inscribed with divers holy texts; and he there performed many Buddhist services on behalf of the spirits of Aoyagi and of her parents.

THE STORY OF MING-Y

THE ANCIENT WORDS OF KOUEI—MASTER OF
MUSICIANS IN THE COURTS OF THE EMPEROR YAO:—

*When ye make to resound the stone melodious, the
Ming-Khieou—When ye touch the lyre that is called
Kin, or the guitar that is called Ssé—Accompanying
their sound with song—Then do the grandfather and
the father return;*

Then do the ghosts of the ancestors come to hear.

*Sang the Poet Tching-Kou: "Surely the Peach-Flowers
blossom over the tomb of Sië-Thao."*

Do you ask me who she was—the beautiful Sië-Thao? For a thousand years and more the trees have been whispering above her bed of stone. And the syllables of her name come to the listener with the lisping of the leaves; with the quivering of many-fingered boughs; with the fluttering of lights and shadows; with the breath, sweet as a woman's presence, of numberless savage flowers—*Sië-Thao*. But, saving the whispering of her name, what the trees say cannot be understood; and they alone remember the years of Sië-Thao. Something about her you might, nevertheless, learn from any of those *Kiang-kou-jin*—those famous Chinese story-tellers, who nightly narrate to listening crowds, in consideration of a few *tsien*, the legends of the past. Something concerning her you may also find in the book entitled "Kin-Kou-Ki-Koan," which signifies in our tongue: "The Marvellous Happenings of Ancient and of Recent Times." And perhaps of all things therein written, the most marvellous is this memory of Sië-Thao:—

Five hundred years ago, in the reign of the Emperor Houng-Wou, whose dynasty was *Ming*, there lived in the City of

Genii, the city of Kwang-tchau-fu, a man celebrated for his learning and for his piety, named Tien-Pelou. This Tien-Pelou had one son, a beautiful boy, who for scholarship and for bodily grace and for polite accomplishments had no superior among the youths of his age. And his name was Ming-Y.

Now when the lad was in his eighteenth summer, it came to pass that Pelou, his father, was appointed Inspector of Public Instruction at the city of Tching-tou; and Ming-Y accompanied his parents thither. Near the city of Tching-tou lived a rich man of rank, a high commissioner of the government, whose name was Tchang, and who wanted to find a worthy teacher for his children. On hearing of the arrival of the new Inspector of Public Instruction, the noble Tchang visited him to obtain advice in this matter; and happening to meet and converse with Pelou's accomplished son, immediately engaged Ming-Y as a private tutor for his family.

Now as the house of this Lord Tchang was situated several miles from town, it was deemed best that Ming-Y should abide in the house of his employer. Accordingly the youth made ready all things necessary for his new sojourn; and his parents, bidding him farewell, counseled him wisely, and cited to him the words of Lao-tseu and of the ancient sages:

"By a beautiful face the world is filled with love; but Heaven may never be deceived thereby. Shouldst thou behold a woman coming from the East, look thou to the West; shouldst thou perceive a maiden approaching from the West, turn thine eyes to the East."

If Ming-Y did not heed this counsel in after days, it was only because of his youth and the thoughtlessness of a naturally joyous heart.

And he departed to abide in the house of Lord Tchang, while the autumn passed, and the winter also.

When the time of the second moon of spring was drawing near, and that happy day which the Chinese call *Hoa-tchao*, or, "The

Birthday of a Hundred Flowers," a longing came upon Ming-Y to
see his parents; and he opened his heart to the good Tchang,
who not only gave him the permission he desired, but also
pressed into his hand a silver gift of two ounces, thinking that
the lad might wish to bring some little memento to his father
and mother. For it is the Chinese custom, on the feast of Hoa-tchao,
to make presents to friends and relations.

That day all the air was drowsy with blossom perfume, and
vibrant with the droning of bees. It seemed to Ming-Y that the
path he followed had not been trodden by any other for many
long years; the grass was tall upon it; vast trees on either side
interlocked their mighty and moss-grown arms above him,
beshadowing the way; but the leafy obscurities quivered with
bird-song, and the deep vistas of the wood were glorified by
vapors of gold, and odorous with flower-breathings as a temple
with incense. The dreamy joy of the day entered into the heart
of Ming-Y; and he sat him down among the young blossoms,
under the branches swaying against the violet sky, to drink in
the perfume and the light, and to enjoy the great sweet silence.
Even while thus reposing, a sound caused him to turn his eyes
toward a shady place where wild peach-trees were in bloom;
and he beheld a young woman, beautiful as the pinkening blossoms themselves, trying to hide among them. Though he looked
for a moment only, Ming-Y could not avoid discerning the loveliness of her face, the golden purity of her complexion, and the
brightness of her long eyes, that sparkled under a pair of brows
as daintily curved as the wings of the silkworm butterfly
outspread. Ming-Y at once turned his gaze away, and, rising quickly,
proceeded on his journey. But so much embarrassed did he feel
at the idea of those charming eyes peeping at him through the
leaves, that he suffered the money he had been carrying in his
sleeve to fall, without being aware of it. A few moments later he
heard the patter of light feet running behind him, and a woman's
voice calling him by name. Turning his face in great surprise, he
saw a comely servant-maid, who said to him, "Sir, my mistress

bade me pick up and return you this silver which you dropped upon the road." Ming-Y thanked the girl gracefully, and requested her to convey his compliments to her mistress. Then he proceeded on his way through the perfumed silence, athwart the shadows that dreamed along the forgotten path, dreaming himself also, and feeling his heart beating with strange quickness at the thought of the beautiful being that he had seen.

It was just such another day when Ming-Y, returning by the same path, paused once more at the spot where the gracious figure had momentarily appeared before him. But this time he was surprised to perceive, through a long vista of immense trees, a dwelling that had previously escaped his notice—a country residence, not large, yet elegant to an unusual degree. The bright blue tiles of its curved and serrated double roof, rising above the foliage, seemed to blend their color with the luminous azure of the day; the green-and-gold designs of its carven porticos were exquisite artistic mockeries of leaves and flowers bathed in sunshine. And at the summit of terrace-steps before it, guarded by great porcelain tortoises, Ming-Y saw standing the mistress of the mansion—the idol of his passionate fancy—accompanied by the same waiting-maid who had borne to her his message of gratitude. While Ming-Y looked, he perceived that their eyes were upon him; they smiled and conversed together as if speaking about him; and, shy though he was, the youth found courage to salute the fair one from a distance. To his astonishment, the young servant beckoned him to approach; and opening a rustic gate half veiled by trailing plants bearing crimson flowers, Ming-Y advanced along the verdant alley leading to the terrace, with mingled feelings of surprise and timid joy. As he drew near, the beautiful lady withdrew from sight; but the maid waited at the broad steps to receive him, and said as he ascended:

"Sir, my mistress understands you wish to thank her for the trifling service she recently bade me do you, and requests that you will enter the house, as she knows you already by repute, and desires to have the pleasure of bidding you good-day."

Ming-Y entered bashfully, his feet making no sound upon a matting elastically soft as forest moss, and found himself in a reception-chamber vast, cool, and fragrant with scent of blossoms freshly gathered. A delicious quiet pervaded the mansion; shadows of flying birds passed over the bands of light that fell through the half-blinds of bamboo; great butterflies, with pinions of fiery color, found their way in, to hover a moment about the painted vases, and pass out again into the mysterious woods. And noiselessly as they, the young mistress of the mansion entered by another door, and kindly greeted the boy, who lifted his hands to his breast and bowed low in salutation. She was taller than he had deemed her, and supplely-slender as a beauteous lily; her black hair was interwoven with the creamy blossoms of the *chu-sha-kih*; her robes of pale silk took shifting tints when she moved, as vapors change hue with the changing of the light.

"If I be not mistaken," she said, when both had seated themselves after having exchanged the customary formalities of politeness, "my honored visitor is none other than Tien-chou, surnamed Ming-Y, educator of the children of my respected relative, the High Commissioner Tchang. As the family of Lord Tchang is my family also, I cannot but consider the teacher of his children as one of my own kin."

"Lady," replied Ming-Y, not a little astonished, "may I dare to inquire the name of your honored family, and to ask the relation which you hold to my noble patron?"

"The name of my poor family," responded the comely lady, "is *Ping*—an ancient family of the city of Tching-tou. I am the daughter of a certain Sië of Moun-hao; Sië is my name, likewise; and I was married to a young man of the Ping family, whose name was Khang. By this marriage I became related to your excellent patron; but my husband died soon after our wedding, and I have chosen this solitary place to reside in during the period of my widowhood."

There was a drowsy music in her voice, as of the melody of brooks, the murmurings of spring; and such a strange grace in the manner of her speech as Ming-Y had never heard before. Yet, on learning that she was a widow, the youth would not have presumed to remain long in her presence without a formal invitation; and after having sipped the cup of rich tea presented to him, he arose to depart. Sië would not suffer him to go so quickly.

"Nay, friend," she said; "stay yet a little while in my house, I pray you; for, should your honored patron ever learn that you had been here, and that I had not treated you as a respected guest, and regaled you even as I would him, I know that he would be greatly angered. Remain at least to supper."

So Ming-Y remained, rejoicing secretly in his heart, for Sië seemed to him the fairest and sweetest being he had ever known, and he felt that he loved her even more than his father and his mother. And while they talked the long shadows of the evening slowly blended into one violet darkness; the great citron-light of the sunset faded out; and those starry beings that are called the Three Councillors, who preside over life and death and the destinies of men, opened their cold bright eyes in the northern sky. Within the mansion of Sië the painted lanterns were lighted; the table was laid for the evening repast; and Ming-Y took his place at it, feeling little inclination to eat, and thinking only of the charming face before him. Observing that he scarcely tasted the dainties laid upon his plate, Sië pressed her young guest to partake of wine; and they drank several cups together. It was a purple wine, so cool that the cup into which it was poured became covered with vapory dew; yet it seemed to warm the veins with strange fire. To Ming-Y, as he drank, all things became more luminous as by enchantment; the walls of the chamber appeared to recede, and the roof to heighten; the lamps glowed like stars in their chains, and the voice of Sië floated to the boy's ears like some far melody heard through the spaces of a drowsy night. His heart swelled; his tongue loosened; and words flitted from his lips that he had fancied he could never dare to utter. Yet Sië sought not to restrain him; her lips gave no smile; but her long bright eyes seemed to laugh with pleasure at his words of praise, and to return his gaze of passionate admiration with affectionate interest.

"I have heard," she said, "of your rare talent, and of your many elegant accomplishments. I know how to sing a little, although I cannot claim to possess any musical learning; and now that I have the honor of finding myself in the society of a musical professor, I will venture to lay modesty aside, and beg you to sing a few songs with me. I should deem it no small gratification if you would condescend to examine my musical compositions."

"The honor and the gratification, dear lady," replied Ming-Y, "will be mine; and I feel helpless to express the gratitude which the offer of so rare a favor deserves."

The serving-maid, obedient to the summons of a little silver gong, brought in the music and retired. Ming-Y took the manuscripts, and began to examine them with eager delight. The paper upon which they were written had a pale yellow tint, and was light as a fabric of gossamer; but the characters were antiquely beautiful, as though they had been traced by the brush of Heï-song Ché-Tchoo himself—that divine Genius of Ink, who is no bigger than a fly; and the signatures attached to the compositions were the signatures of Youen-tchin, Kao-pien, and Thou-mou—mighty poets and musicians of the dynasty of Thang! Ming-Y could not repress a scream of delight at the sight of treasures so inestimable and so unique; scarcely could he summon resolution enough to permit them to leave his hands even for a moment. "O Lady!" he cried, "these are veritably priceless things, surpassing in worth the treasures of all kings. This indeed is the handwriting of those great masters who sang five hundred years before our birth. How marvellously it has been preserved! Is not this the wondrous ink of which it was written: *Po-nien-jou-chi, i-tien-jou-ki*—'After centuries I remain firm as stone, and the letters that I make like lacquer'? And how divine the charm of this composition!—the song of Kao-pien, prince of poets, and Governor of Sze-tchouen five hundred years ago!"

"Kao-pien! darling Kao-pien!" murmured Sië, with a singular light in her eyes. "Kao-pien is also my favorite. Dear Ming-Y, let us chant his verses together, to the melody of old—the music of those grand years when men were nobler and wiser than to-day."

And their voices rose through the perfumed night like the voices of the wonder-birds—of the Fung-hoang—blending together in liquid sweetness. Yet a moment, and Ming-Y, overcome by the witchery of his companion's voice, could only listen in speechless ecstasy, while the lights of the chamber swam dim before his sight, and tears of pleasure trickled down his cheeks.

So the ninth hour passed; and they continued to converse, and to drink the cool purple wine, and to sing the songs of the years of Thang, until far into the night. More than once Ming-Y thought of departing; but each time Sië would begin, in that silver-sweet voice of hers, so wondrous a story of the great poets of the past, and of the women whom they loved, that he became as one entranced; or she would sing for him a song so strange that all his senses seemed to die except that of hearing. And at last, as she paused to pledge him in a cup of wine, Ming-Y could not restrain himself from putting his arm about her round neck and drawing her dainty head closer to him, and kissing the lips that were so much ruddier and sweeter than the wine. Then their lips separated no more;—the night grew old, and they knew it not.

The birds awakened, the flowers opened their eyes to the rising sun, and Ming-Y found himself at last compelled to bid his lovely enchantress farewell. Sië, accompanying him to the terrace, kissed him fondly and said, "Dear boy, come hither as often as you are able—as often as your heart whispers you to come. I know that you are not of those without faith and truth, who betray secrets; yet, being so young, you might also be sometimes thoughtless; and I pray you never to forget that only the stars have been the witnesses of our love. Speak of it to no living person, dearest; and take with you this little souvenir of our happy night."

And she presented him with an exquisite and curious little thing—a paper-weight in likeness of a couchant lion, wrought from a jade-stone yellow as that created by a rainbow in honor of Kong-fu-tze. Tenderly the boy kissed the gift and the beautiful hand that gave it. "May the Spirits punish me," he vowed, "if ever I knowingly give you cause to reproach me, sweetheart!" And they separated with mutual vows.

That morning, on returning to the house of Lord Tchang, Ming-Y told the first falsehood which had ever passed his lips. He averred that his mother had requested him thenceforward to pass his nights at home, now that the weather had become so pleasant; for, though the way was somewhat long, he was strong and active, and needed both air and healthy exercise. Tchang believed all Ming-Y said, and offered no objection. Accordingly the lad found himself enabled to pass all his evenings at the house of the beautiful Sië. Each night they devoted to the same pleasures which had made their first acquaintance so charming: they sang and conversed by turns; they played at chess—the learned game invented by Wu-Wang, which is an imitation of war; they composed pieces of eighty rhymes upon the flowers, the trees, the clouds, the streams, the birds, the bees. But in all accomplishments Sië far excelled her young sweetheart. Whenever they played at chess, it was always Ming-Y's general, Ming-Y's *tsiang*, who was surrounded and vanquished; when they composed verses, Sië's poems were ever superior to his in harmony of word-coloring, in elegance of form, in classic loftiness of thought. And the themes they selected were always the most difficult—those of the poets of the Thang dynasty; the songs they sang were also the songs of five hundred years before—the songs of Youen-tchin, of Thou-mou, of Kao-pien above all, high poet and ruler of the province of Sze-tchouen.

So the summer waxed and waned upon their love, and the luminous autumn came, with its vapors of phantom gold, its shadows of magical purple.

Then it unexpectedly happened that the father of Ming-Y, meeting his son's employer at Tching-tou, was asked by him: "Why must your boy continue to travel every evening to the city, now that the winter is approaching? The way is long, and when he returns in the morning he looks fordone with weariness. Why not permit him to slumber in my house during the season of snow?" And the father of Ming-Y, greatly astonished, responded: "Sir, my son has not visited the city, nor has he been to our house all this summer. I fear that he must have acquired wicked habits, and that he passes his nights in evil company—perhaps in gaming, or in drinking with the women of the flower-boats." But the High Commissioner returned: "Nay! that is not to be thought of. I have never found any evil in the boy, and there are no taverns nor flower-boats nor any places of dissipation in our neighborhood. No doubt Ming-Y has found some amiable youth of his own age with whom to spend his evenings, and only told me an untruth for fear that I would not otherwise permit him to leave my residence. I beg that you will say nothing to him until I shall have sought to discover this mystery; and this very evening I shall send my servant to follow after him, and to watch whither he goes."

Pelou readily assented to this proposal, and promising to visit Tchang the following morning, returned to his home. In the evening, when Ming-Y left the house of Tchang, a servant followed him unobserved at a distance. But on reaching the most obscure portion of the road, the boy disappeared from sight as suddenly as though the earth had swallowed him. After having long sought after him in vain, the domestic returned in great bewilderment to the house, and related what had taken place. Tchang immediately sent a messenger to Pelou.

In the meantime Ming-Y, entering the chamber of his beloved, was surprised and deeply pained to find her in tears. "Sweetheart," she sobbed, wreathing her arms around his neck, "we are about to be separated forever, because of reasons which I cannot tell you. From the very first I knew this must come to pass; and nevertheless it seemed to me for the moment so cruelly sudden a loss, so unexpected a misfortune, that I could not prevent myself from weeping! After this night we shall never see each other again, beloved, and I know that you will not be able to forget me while you live; but I know also that you will become a great scholar, and that honors and riches will be showered upon you, and that some beautiful and loving woman will console you for my loss. And now let us speak no more of grief; but let us pass this last evening joyously, so that your recollection of me may not be a painful one, and that you may remember my laughter rather than my tears."

She brushed the bright drops away, and brought wine and music and the melodious *kin* of seven silken strings, and would not suffer Ming-Y to speak for one moment of the coming separation. And she sang him an ancient song about the calmness of summer lakes reflecting the blue of heaven only, and the calmness of the heart also, before the clouds of care and of grief and of weariness darken its little world. Soon they forgot their sorrow in the joy of song and wine; and those last hours seemed to Ming-Y more celestial than even the hours of their first bliss.

But when the yellow beauty of morning came their sadness returned, and they wept. Once more Sië accompanied her lover to the terrace-steps; and as she kissed him farewell, she pressed into his hand a parting gift—a little brush-case of agate, wonderfully chiseled, and worthy the table of a great poet. And they separated forever, shedding many tears.

Still Ming-Y could not believe it was an eternal parting. "No!" he thought, "I shall visit her tomorrow; for I cannot now live without her, and I feel assured that she cannot refuse to receive me." Such were the thoughts that filled his mind as he reached the house of Tchang, to find his father and his patron standing on the porch awaiting him. Ere he could speak a word, Pelou demanded: "Son, in what place have you been passing your nights?"

Seeing that his falsehood had been discovered, Ming-Y dared not make any reply, and remained abashed and silent, with bowed head, in the presence of his father. Then Pelou, striking the boy violently with his staff, commanded him to divulge the secret; and at last, partly through fear of his parent, and partly through fear of the law which ordains that "*the son refusing to obey his father shall be punished with one hundred blows of the bamboo,*" Ming-Y faltered out the history of his love.

Tchang changed color at the boy's tale. "Child," exclaimed the High Commissioner, "I have no relative of the name of Ping; I have never heard of the woman you describe; I have never heard even of the house which you speak of. But I know also that you cannot dare to lie to Pelou, your honored father; there is some strange delusion in all this affair."

Then Ming-Y produced the gifts that Sië had given him—the lion of yellow jade, the brush-case of carven agate, also some original compositions made by the beautiful lady herself. The astonishment of Tchang was now shared by Pelou. Both observed that the brush-case of agate and the lion of jade bore the appearance of objects that had lain buried in the earth for centuries, and were of a workmanship beyond the power of living man to imitate; while the compositions proved to be veritable master-pieces of poetry, written in the style of the poets of the dynasty of Thang.

"Friend Pelou," cried the High Commissioner, "let us immediately accompany the boy to the place where he obtained these miraculous things, and apply the testimony of our senses to this mystery. The boy is no doubt telling the truth; yet his story passes my understanding." And all three proceeded toward the place of the habitation of Sië.

But when they had arrived at the shadiest part of the road, where the perfumes were most sweet and the mosses were greenest, and the fruits of the wild peach flushed most pinkly, Ming-Y, gazing through the groves, uttered a cry of dismay. Where the azure-tiled roof had risen against the sky, there was now only the blue emptiness of air; where the green-and-gold facade had been, there was visible only the flickering of leaves under the aureate autumn light; and where the broad terrace had extended, could be discerned only a ruin—a tomb so ancient, so deeply gnawed by moss, that the name graven upon it was no longer decipherable. The home of Sië had disappeared!

All suddenly the High Commissioner smote his forehead with his hand, and turning to Pelou, recited the well-known verse of the ancient poet Tching-Kou:—

"Surely the peach-flowers blossom over the tomb of sië-thao."

"Friend Pelou," continued Tchang, "the beauty who bewitched your son was no other than she whose tomb stands there in ruin before us! Did she not say she was wedded to Ping-Khang? There is no family of that name, but Ping-Khang is indeed the name of a broad alley in the city near. There was a dark riddle in all that she said. She called herself Sië of Moun-Hiao: there is no person of that name; there is no street of that name; but the Chinese characters *Moun* and *hiao*, placed together, form the character 'Kiao.' Listen! The alley Ping-Khang, situated in the street Kiao, was the place where dwelt the great courtesans of the dynasty of Thang! Did she not sing the songs of Kao-pien? And upon the brush-case and the paper-weight she gave your son, are there not characters which read, '*Pure object of art belonging to Kao, of the city of Pho-hai*'? That city no longer exists; but the memory of Kao-pien remains, for he was governor of the province of Sze-tchouen, and a mighty poet. And when he dwelt in the land of Chou, was not his favorite the beautiful wanton Sië—Sië-Thao, unmatched for grace among all the women of her day? It was he who made her a gift of those manuscripts of song; it was he who gave her those objects of rare art. Sië-Thao died not as other women die. Her limbs may have crumbled to dust; yet something of her still lives in this deep wood—her Shadow still haunts this shadowy place."

Tchang ceased to speak. A vague fear fell upon the three. The thin mists of the morning made dim the distances of green, and deepened the ghostly beauty of the woods. A faint breeze passed by, leaving a trail of blossom-scent—a last odor of dying flowers—

thin as that which clings to the silk of a forgotten robe; and, as it passed, the trees seemed to whisper across the silence, "*Sië-Thao.*"

Fearing greatly for his son, Pelou sent the lad away at once to the city of Kwang-tchau-fu. And there, in after years, Ming-Y obtained high dignities and honors by reason of his talents and his learning; and he married the daughter of an illustrious house, by whom he became the father of sons and daughters famous for their virtues and their accomplishments. Never could he forget Sië-Thao; and yet it is said that he never spoke of her—not even when his children begged him to tell them the story of two beautiful objects that always lay upon his writing-table: a lion of yellow jade, and a brush-case of carven agate.

THE STORY OF O-TEI

A long time ago, in the town of Niigata, in the province of Echizen, there lived a man called Nagao Chosei.

Nagao was the son of a physician, and was educated for his father's profession. At an early age he had been betrothed to a girl called O-Tei, the daughter of one of his father's friends; and both families had agreed that the wedding should take place as soon as Nagao had finished his studies. But the health of O-Tei proved to be weak; and in her fifteenth year she was attacked by a fatal consumption. When she became aware that she must die, she sent for Nagao to bid him farewell.

As he knelt at her bedside, she said to him:—

"Nagao-Sama,[23] my betrothed, we were promised to each other from the time of our childhood; and we were to have been married at the end of this year. But now I am going to die;—the gods know what is best for us. If I were able to live for some years longer, I could only continue to be a cause of trouble and grief for others. With this frail body, I could not be a good wife; and therefore even to wish to live, for your sake, would be a very selfish wish. I am quite resigned to die; and I want you to promise that you will not grieve... Besides, I want to tell you that I think we shall meet again."...

"Indeed we shall meet again," Nagao answered earnestly. "And in that Pure Land[24] there will be no pain of separation."

"Nay, nay!" she responded softly, "I meant not the Pure Land. I believe that we are destined to meet again in this world—although I shall be buried to-morrow."

Nagao looked at her wonderingly, and saw her smile at his wonder. She continued, in her gentle, dreamy voice—

"Yes, I mean in this world—in your own present life, Nagao-Sama... Providing, indeed, that you wish it. Only, for this

23   "Sama" is a polite suffix attached to personal names.

24   A Buddhist term commonly used to signify a kind of heaven.

thing to happen, I must again be born a girl, and grow up to womanhood. So you would have to wait. Fifteen—sixteen years: that is a long time... But, my promised husband, you are now only nineteen years old."...

Eager to soothe her dying moments, he answered tenderly:—

"To wait for you, my betrothed, were no less a joy than a duty. We are pledged to each other for the time of seven existences."

"But you doubt?" she questioned, watching his face.

"My dear one," he answered, "I doubt whether I should be able to know you in another body, under another name—unless you can tell me of a sign or token."

"That I cannot do," she said. "Only the Gods and the Buddhas know how and where we shall meet. But I am sure—very, very sure—that, if you be not unwilling to receive me, I shall be able to come back to you... Remember these words of mine."...

She ceased to speak; and her eyes closed. She was dead.

Nagao had been sincerely attached to O-Tei; and his grief was deep. He had a mortuary tablet made, inscribed with her zokumyō;[25] and he placed the tablet in his *butsudan*,[26] and every day set offerings before it. He thought a great deal about the strange things that O-Tei had said to him just before her death; and, in the hope of pleasing her spirit, he wrote a solemn promise to wed her if she could ever return to him in another body. This written promise he sealed with his seal, and placed in the *butsudan* beside the mortuary tablet of O-Tei.

25　The Buddhist term zokumyō ("profane name") signifies the personal name, borne during life, in contradistinction to the kaimyō ("sila-name") or homyō ("law-name") given after death—religious post-humous appellations inscribed upon the tomb, and upon the mortuary tablet in the parish-temple. For some account of these, see my paper entitled, "The Literature of the Dead," in *Exotics and Retrospectives*.

26　Buddhist household shrine.

Nevertheless, as Nagao was an only son, it was necessary that he should marry. He soon found himself obliged to yield to the wishes of his family, and to accept a wife of his father's choosing. After his marriage he continued to set offerings before the tablet of O-Tei; and he never failed to remember her with affection. But by degrees her image became dim in his memory—like a dream that is hard to recall. And the years went by.

During those years many misfortunes came upon him. He lost his parents by death—then his wife and his only child. So that he found himself alone in the world. He abandoned his desolate home, and set out upon a long journey in the hope of forgetting his sorrows.

One day, in the course of his travels, he arrived at Ikao—a mountain-village still famed for its thermal springs, and for the beautiful scenery of its neighborhood. In the village-inn at which he stopped, a young girl came to wait upon him; and, at the first sight of her face, he felt his heart leap as it had never leaped before. So strangely did she resemble O-Tei that he pinched himself to make sure that he was not dreaming. As she went and came—bringing fire and food, or arranging the chamber of the guest—her every attitude and motion revived in him some gracious memory of the girl to whom he had been pledged in his youth. He spoke to her; and she responded in a soft, clear voice of which the sweetness saddened him with a sadness of other days.

Then, in great wonder, he questioned her, saying:—

"Elder Sister,[27] so much do you look like a person whom I knew long ago, that I was startled when you first entered this room. Pardon me, therefore, for asking what is your native place, and what is your name?"

Immediately—and in the unforgotten voice of the dead—she thus made answer:—

"My name is O-Tei; and you are Nagao Chosei of Echigo, my promised husband. Seventeen years ago, I died in Niigata: then

---

27   Direct translation of a Japanese form of address used toward young, unmarried women.

you made in writing a promise to marry me if ever I could come back to this world in the body of a woman;—and you sealed that written promise with your seal, and put it in the *butsudan*, beside the tablet inscribed with my name. And therefore I came back."...

As she uttered these last words, she fell unconscious.

Nagao married her; and the marriage was a happy one. But at no time afterwards could she remember what she had told him in answer to his question at Ikao: neither could she remember anything of her previous existence. The recollection of the former birth—mysteriously kindled in the moment of that meeting—had again become obscured, and so thereafter remained.

ROKURO-KUBI

Nearly five hundred years ago there was a samurai, named Isogai Heidazaemon Taketsura, in the service of the Lord Kikuji, of Kyūshū. This Isogai had inherited, from many warlike ancestors, a natural aptitude for military exercises, and extraordinary strength. While yet a boy he had surpassed his teachers in the art of swordsmanship, in archery, and in the use of the spear, and had displayed all the capacities of a daring and skillful soldier. Afterwards, in the time of the Eikyō[28] war, he so distinguished himself that high honors were bestowed upon him. But when the house of Kikuji came to ruin, Isogai found himself without a master. He might then easily have obtained service under another daimyo; but as he had never sought distinction for his own sake alone, and as his heart remained true to his former lord, he preferred to give up the world. So he cut off his hair, and became a traveling priest—taking the Buddhist name of Kwairyo.

But always, under the *koromo*[29] of the priest, Kwairyo kept warm within him the heart of the samurai. As in other years he had laughed at peril, so now also he scorned danger; and in all weathers and all seasons he journeyed to preach the good Law in places where no other priest would have dared to go. For that age was an age of violence and disorder; and upon the highways there was no security for the solitary traveler, even if he happened to be a priest.

In the course of his first long journey, Kwairyo had occasion to visit the province of Kai. One evening, as he was traveling through the mountains of that province, darkness overcame him in a very lonesome district, leagues away from any village. So he resigned himself to pass the night under the stars; and having found a suitable grassy spot, by the roadside, he lay down there,

---

28   The period of Eikyō lasted from 1429 to 1441.

29   The upper robe of a Buddhist priest is thus called.

and prepared to sleep. He had always welcomed discomfort; and even a bare rock was for him a good bed, when nothing better could be found, and the root of a pine-tree an excellent pillow. His body was iron; and he never troubled himself about dews or rain or frost or snow.

Scarcely had he lain down when a man came along the road, carrying an axe and a great bundle of chopped wood. This woodcutter halted on seeing Kwairyo lying down, and, after a moment of silent observation, said to him in a tone of great surprise:—

"What kind of a man can you be, good Sir, that you dare to lie down alone in such a place as this?...There are haunters about here—many of them. Are you not afraid of Hairy Things?"

"My friend," cheerfully answered Kwairyo, "I am only a wandering priest—a 'Cloud-and-Water-Guest,' as folks call it: *Unsui-no-ryokaku*.[30] And I am not in the least afraid of Hairy Things—if you mean goblin-foxes, or goblin-badgers, or any creatures of that kind. As for lonesome places, I like them: they are suitable for meditation. I am accustomed to sleeping in the open air: and I have learned never to be anxious about my life."

"You must be indeed a brave man, Sir Priest," the peasant responded, "to lie down here! This place has a bad name—a very bad name. But, as the proverb has it, *Kunshi ayayuki ni chikayorazu* ['The superior man does not needlessly expose himself to peril']; and I must assure you, Sir, that it is very dangerous to sleep here. Therefore, although my house is only a wretched thatched hut, let me beg of you to come home with me at once. In the way of food, I have nothing to offer you; but there is a roof at least, and you can sleep under it without risk."

He spoke earnestly; and Kwairyo, liking the kindly tone of the man, accepted this modest offer. The woodcutter guided him along a narrow path, leading up from the main road through mountain–forest. It was a rough and dangerous path—sometimes skirting precipices—sometimes offering nothing but a network

---

30   A term for itinerant priests.

of slippery roots for the foot to rest upon—sometimes winding over or between masses of jagged rock. But at last Kwairyo found himself upon a cleared space at the top of a hill, with a full moon shining overhead; and he saw before him a small thatched cottage, cheerfully lighted from within. The woodcutter led him to a shed at the back of the house, whither water had been conducted, through bamboo-pipes, from some neighboring stream; and the two men washed their feet. Beyond the shed was a vegetable garden, and a grove of cedars and bamboos; and beyond the trees appeared the glimmer of a cascade, pouring from some loftier height, and swaying in the moonshine like a long white robe.

As Kwairyo entered the cottage with his guide, he perceived four persons—men and women—warming their hands at a little fire kindled in the *ro*[31] of the principle apartment. They bowed low to the priest, and greeted him in the most respectful manner. Kwairyo wondered that persons so poor, and dwelling in such a solitude, should be aware of the polite forms of greeting. "These are good people," he thought to himself; "and they must have been taught by someone well acquainted with the rules of propriety." Then turning to his host—the *aruji*, or house-master, as the others called him—Kwairyo said:—

"From the kindness of your speech, and from the very polite welcome given me by your household, I imagine that you have not always been a woodcutter. Perhaps you formerly belonged to one of the upper classes?"

Smiling, the woodcutter answered:—

"Sir, you are not mistaken. Though now living as you find me, I was once a person of some distinction. My story is the story of a ruined life—ruined by my own fault. I used to be in the service of a daimyo; and my rank in that service was not inconsiderable. But I loved women and wine too well; and under

---

31   A sort of little fireplace, contrived in the floor of a room, is thus described. The *ro* is usually a square shallow cavity, lined with metal and half-filled with ashes, in which charcoal is lighted.

the influence of passion I acted wickedly. My selfishness brought about the ruin of our house, and caused the death of many persons. Retribution followed me; and I long remained a fugitive in the land. Now I often pray that I may be able to make some atonement for the evil which I did, and to re-establish the ancestral home. But I fear that I shall never find any way of so doing. Nevertheless, I try to overcome the karma of my errors by sincere repentance, and by helping as far as I can, those who are unfortunate."

Kwairyo was pleased by this announcement of good resolve; and he said to the *aruji*:—

"My friend, I have had occasion to observe that man, prone to folly in their youth, may in after years become very earnest in right living. In the holy sutras it is written that those strongest in wrong-doing can become, by power of good resolve, the strongest in right-doing. I do not doubt that you have a good heart; and I hope that better fortune will come to you. To-night I shall recite the sutras for your sake, and pray that you may obtain the force to overcome the karma of any past errors."

With these assurances, Kwairyo bade the *aruji* good-night; and his host showed him to a very small side-room, where a bed had been made ready. Then all went to sleep except the priest, who began to read the sutras by the light of a paper lantern. Until a late hour he continued to read and pray: then he opened a little window in his little sleeping-room, to take a last look at the landscape before lying down. The night was beautiful: there was no cloud in the sky: there was no wind; and the strong moonlight threw down sharp black shadows of foliage, and glittered on the dews of the garden. Shrillings of crickets and bell-insects[32] made a musical tumult; and the sound of the neighboring cascade deepened with the night. Kwairyo felt thirsty as he listened to the noise of the water; and, remembering the bamboo aqueduct at the rear of the house, he thought that he

---

32   Direct translation of "*suzumushi*," a kind of cricket with a distinctive chirp like a tiny bell, whence the name.

could go there and get a drink without disturbing the sleeping household. Very gently he pushed apart the sliding-screens that separated his room from the main apartment; and he saw, by the light of the lantern, five recumbent bodies—without heads!

For one instant he stood bewildered—imagining a crime. But in another moment he perceived that there was no blood, and that the headless necks did not look as if they had been cut. Then he thought to himself:—"Either this is an illusion made by goblins, or I have been lured into the dwelling of a Rokuro-Kubi...[33] In the book *Soshinki*[34] it is written that if one find the body of a Rokuro-Kubi without its head, and remove the body to another place, the head will never be able to join itself again to the neck. And the book further says that when the head comes back and finds that its body has been moved, it will strike itself upon the floor three times—bounding like a ball—and will pant as in great fear, and presently die. Now, if these be Rokuro-Kubi, they mean me no good;—so I shall be justified in following the instructions of the book."...

He seized the body of the *aruji* by the feet, pulled it to the window, and pushed it out. Then he went to the back-door, which he found barred; and he surmised that the heads had made their exit through the smoke-hole in the roof, which had been left open. Gently unbarring the door, he made his way to the garden, and proceeded with all possible caution to the grove beyond it. He heard voices talking in the grove; and he went in the direction of the voices—stealing from shadow to shadow, until he reached a good hiding-place. Then, from behind a trunk, he caught sight of the heads—all five of them—flitting about, and chatting as they flitted. They were eating worms and insects which they found on the ground or among the trees. Presently the head of the *aruji* stopped eating and said:—

33   Now a rokuro-kubi is ordinarily conceived as a goblin whose neck stretches out to great lengths, but which nevertheless always remains attached to its body.

34   A Chinese collection of stories on the supernatural.

"Ah, that traveling priest who came to-night!—how fat all his body is! When we shall have eaten him, our bellies will be well filled... I was foolish to talk to him as I did;—it only set him to reciting the sutras on behalf of my soul! To go near him while he is reciting would be difficult; and we cannot touch him so long as he is praying. But as it is now nearly morning, perhaps he has gone to sleep... Some one of you go to the house and see what the fellow is doing."

Another head—the head of a young woman—immediately rose up and flitted to the house, lightly as a bat. After a few minutes it came back, and cried out huskily, in a tone of great alarm:—

"That traveling priest is not in the house;—he is gone! But that is not the worst of the matter. He has taken the body of our *aruji*; and I do not know where he has put it."

At this announcement the head of the *aruji*—distinctly visible in the moonlight—assumed a frightful aspect: its eyes opened monstrously; its hair stood up bristling; and its teeth gnashed. Then a cry burst from its lips; and—weeping tears of rage—it exclaimed:—

"Since my body has been moved, to rejoin it is not possible! Then I must die!...And all through the work of that priest! Before I die I will get at that priest!—I will tear him!—I will devour him!... and there he is—behind that tree!—hiding behind that tree! See him!—the fat coward!"...

In the same moment the head of the *aruji*, followed by the other four heads, sprang at Kwairyo. But the strong priest had already armed himself by plucking up a young tree; and with that tree he struck the heads as they came—knocking them from him with tremendous blows. Four of them fled away. But the head of the *aruji*, though battered again and again, desperately continued to bound at the priest, and at last caught him by the left sleeve of his robe. Kwairyo, however, as quickly gripped the head by its topknot, and repeatedly struck it. It did not release its hold; but it uttered a long moan, and thereafter ceased to struggle. It was dead. But its teeth still held the sleeve; and, for all his great strength, Kwairyo could not force open the jaws.

With the head still hanging to his sleeve he went back to the house, and there caught sight of the other four Rokuro-Kubi squatting together, with their bruised and bleeding heads reunited to their bodies. But when they perceived him at the back-door all screamed, "The priest! The priest!"—and fled, through the other doorway, out into the woods.

Eastward the sky was brightening; day was about to dawn; and Kwairyo knew that the power of the goblins was limited to the hours of darkness. He looked at the head clinging to his sleeve— its face all fouled with blood and foam and clay; and he laughed aloud as he thought to himself: "*What a miyage!*[35]—the head of a goblin!" After which he gathered together his few belongings, and leisurely descended the mountain to continue his journey.

Right on he journeyed, until he came to Suwa in Shinano; and into the main street of Suwa he solemnly strode, with the head dangling at his elbow. Then women fainted, and children screamed and ran away; and there was a great crowding and clamoring until the *torite* (as the police in those days were called) seized the priest, and took him to jail. For they supposed the head to be the head of a murdered man who, in the moment of being killed, had caught the murderer's sleeve in his teeth. As for Kwairyo, he only smiled and said nothing when they questioned him. So, after having passed a night in prison, he was brought before the magistrates of the district. Then he was ordered to explain how he, a priest, had been found with the head of a man fastened to his sleeve, and why he had dared thus shamelessly to parade his crime in the sight of people.

Kwairyo laughed long and loudly at these questions; and then he said:—

---

35   A present made to friends or to the household on returning from a journey is thus called. Ordinarily, of course, the *miyage* consists of something produced in the locality to which the journey has been made: this is the point of Kwairyo's jest.

"Sirs, I did not fasten the head to my sleeve: it fastened itself there—much against my will. And I have not committed any crime. For this is not the head of a man; it is the head of a goblin;—and, if I caused the death of the goblin, I did not do so by any shedding of blood, but simply by taking the precautions necessary to assure my own safety.".... And he proceeded to relate the whole of the adventure—bursting into another hearty laugh as he told of his encounter with the five heads.

But the magistrates did not laugh. They judged him to be a hardened criminal, and his story an insult to their intelligence. Therefore, without further questioning, they decided to order his immediate execution—all of them except one, a very old man. This aged officer had made no remark during the trial; but, after having heard the opinion of his colleagues, he rose up, and said:—

"Let us first examine the head carefully; for this, I think, has not yet been done. If the priest has spoken truth, the head itself should bear witness for him... Bring the head here!"

So the head, still holding in its teeth the *koromo* that had been stripped from Kwairyo's shoulders, was put before the judges. The old man turned it round and round, carefully examined it, and discovered, on the nape of its neck, several strange red characters. He called the attention of his colleagues to these, and also bade them observe that the edges of the neck nowhere presented the appearance of having been cut by any weapon. On the contrary, the line of leverance was smooth as the line at which a falling leaf detaches itself from the stem... Then said the elder:—

"I am quite sure that the priest told us nothing but the truth. This is the head of a Rokuro-Kubi. In the book *Nan-ho-i-butsu-shi* it is written that certain red characters can always be found upon the nape of the neck of a real Rokuro-Kubi. There are the characters: you can see for yourselves that they have not been painted. Moreover, it is well known that such goblins have been dwelling in the mountains of the province of Kai from very

ancient time… But you, Sir," he exclaimed, turning to Kwairyo—
"what sort of sturdy priest may you be? Certainly you have given
proof of a courage that few priests possess; and you have the
air of a soldier rather than a priest. Perhaps you once belonged
to the samurai-class?"

"You have guessed rightly, Sir," Kwairyo responded. "Before
becoming a priest, I long followed the profession of arms; and
in those days I never feared man or devil. My name then was
Isogai Heidazaemon Taketsura of Kyūshū: there may be some
among you who remember it."

At the mention of that name, a murmur of admiration filled
the court-room; for there were many present who remembered
it. And Kwairyo immediately found himself among friends instead
of judges—friends anxious to prove their admiration by fraternal
kindness. With honor they escorted him to the residence of the
daimyo, who welcomed him, and feasted him, and made him a
handsome present before allowing him to depart. When Kwairyo
left Suwa, he was as happy as any priest is permitted to be in
this transitory world. As for the head, he took it with him—
jocosely insisting that he intended it for a *miyage*.

And now it only remains to tell what became of the head.

A day or two after leaving Suwa, Kwairyo met with a robber,
who stopped him in a lonesome place, and bade him strip.
Kwairyo at once removed his *koromo*, and offered it to the
robber, who then first perceived what was hanging to the sleeve.
Though brave, the highwayman was startled: he dropped the
garment, and sprang back. Then he cried out:—"You!—what kind
of a priest are you? Why, you are a worse man than I am! It is
true that I have killed people; but I never walked about with
anybody's head fastened to my sleeve… Well, Sir priest, I suppose
we are of the same calling; and I must say that I admire you!…
Now that head would be of use to me: I could frighten people
with it. Will you sell it? You can have my robe in exchange for
your *koromo*; and I will give you five ryō for the head."

Kwairyo answered:—

"I shall let you have the head and the robe if you insist; but I must tell you that this is not the head of a man. It is a goblin's head. So, if you buy it, and have any trouble in consequence, please to remember that you were not deceived by me."

"What a nice priest you are!" exclaimed the robber. "You kill men, and jest about it!... But I am really in earnest. Here is my robe; and here is the money;—and let me have the head... What is the use of joking?"

"Take the thing," said Kwairyo. "I was not joking. The only joke—if there be any joke at all—is that you are fool enough to pay good money for a goblin's head." And Kwairyo, loudly laughing, went upon his way.

Thus the robber got the head and the *koromo*; and for some time he played goblin-priest upon the highways. But, reaching the neighborhood of Suwa, he there leaned the true story of the head; and he then became afraid that the spirit of the Rokuro-Kubi might give him trouble. So he made up his mind to take back the head to the place from which it had come, and to bury it with its body. He found his way to the lonely cottage in the mountains of Kai; but nobody was there, and he could not discover the body. Therefore he buried the head by itself, in the grove behind the cottage; and he had a tombstone set up over the grave; and he caused a *Segaki*-service to be performed on behalf of the spirit of the Rokuro-Kubi. And that tombstone—known as the Tombstone of the Rokuro-Kubi—may be seen (at least so the Japanese story-teller declares) even unto this day.

A DEAD SECRET

Along time ago, in the province of Tamba, there lived a rich merchant named Inamuraya Gensuke. He had a daughter called O-Sono. As she was very clever and pretty, he thought it would be a pity to let her grow up with only such teaching as the country-teachers could give her: so he sent her, in care of some trusty attendants, to Kyoto, that she might be trained in the polite accomplishments taught to the ladies of the capital. After she had thus been educated, she was married to a friend of her father's family—a merchant named Nagaraya;—and she lived happily with him for nearly four years. They had one child—a boy. But O-Sono fell ill and died, in the fourth year after her marriage.

On the night after the funeral of O-Sono, her little son said that his mamma had come back, and was in the room upstairs. She had smiled at him, but would not talk to him: so he became afraid, and ran away. Then some of the family went upstairs to the room which had been O-Sono's; and they were startled to see, by the light of a small lamp which had been kindled before a shrine in that room, the figure of the dead mother. She appeared as if standing in front of a *tansu*, or chest of drawers, that still contained her ornaments and her wearing-apparel. Her head and shoulders could be very distinctly seen; but from the waist downwards the figure thinned into invisibility;—it was like an imperfect reflection of her, and transparent as a shadow on water.

Then the folk were afraid, and left the room. Below they consulted together; and the mother of O-Sono's husband said: "A woman is fond of her small things; and O-Sono was much attached to her belongings. Perhaps she has come back to look at them. Many dead persons will do that—unless the things be given to the parish-temple. If we present O-Sono's robes and girdles to the temple, her spirit will probably find rest."

It was agreed that this should be done as soon as possible. So on the following morning the drawers were emptied; and all of O-Sono's ornaments and dresses were taken to the temple. But she came back the next night, and looked at the *tansu* as before. And she came back also on the night following, and the night after that, and every night;—and the house became a house of fear.

The mother of O-Sono's husband then went to the parish-temple, and told the chief priest all that had happened, and asked for ghostly counsel. The temple was a Zen temple; and the head-priest was a learned old man, known as Daigen Osho. He said: "There must be something about which she is anxious, in or near that *tansu*."—"But we emptied all the drawers," replied the woman;—"there is nothing in the *tansu*."—"Well," said Daigen Osho, "to-night I shall go to your house, and keep watch in that room, and see what can be done. You must give orders that no person shall enter the room while I am watching, unless I call."

After sundown, Daigen Osho went to the house, and found the room made ready for him. He remained there alone, reading the sutras; and nothing appeared until after the Hour of the Rat.[36] Then the figure of O-Sono suddenly outlined itself in front of the *tansu*. Her face had a wistful look; and she kept her eyes fixed upon the *tansu*.

The priest uttered the holy formula prescribed in such cases, and then, addressing the figure by the kaimyō[37] of O-Sono, said:—"I have come here in order to help you. Perhaps in that *tansu* there is something about which you have reason to feel

---

36   The Hour of the Rat (*Ne-no-Koku*), according to the old Japanese method of reckoning time, was the first hour. It corresponded to the time between our midnight and two o'clock in the morning; for the ancient Japanese hours were each equal to two modern hours.

37   Kaimyō, the posthumous Buddhist name, or religious name, given to the dead. Strictly speaking, the meaning of the word is sila-name. (See my paper entitled, "The Literature of the Dead" in *Exotics and Retrospectives*.)

anxious. Shall I try to find it for you?" The shadow appeared to give assent by a slight motion of the head; and the priest, rising, opened the top drawer. It was empty. Successively he opened the second, the third, and the fourth drawer;—he searched carefully behind them and beneath them;—he carefully examined the interior of the chest. He found nothing. But the figure remained gazing as wistfully as before. "What can she want?" thought the priest. Suddenly it occurred to him that there might be something hidden under the paper with which the drawers were lined. He removed the lining of the first drawer:—nothing! He removed the lining of the second and third drawers:—still nothing. But under the lining of the lowermost drawer he found—a letter. "Is this the thing about which you have been troubled?" he asked. The shadow of the woman turned toward him—her faint gaze fixed upon the letter. "Shall I burn it for you?" he asked. She bowed before him. "It shall be burned in the temple this very morning," he promised;—"and no one shall read it, except myself." The figure smiled and vanished.

Dawn was breaking as the priest descended the stairs, to find the family waiting anxiously below. "Do not be anxious," he said to them: "She will not appear again." And she never did.

The letter was burned. It was a love-letter written to O-Sono in the time of her studies at Kyoto. But the priest alone knew what was in it; and the secret died with him.

THE DREAM OF AKINOSUKE

In the district called Toichi of Yamato Province, there used to live a *goshi* named Miyata Akinosuke… [Here I must tell you that in Japanese feudal times there was a privileged class of soldier-farmers—free-holders—corresponding to the class of yeomen in England; and these were called *goshi*.]

In Akinosuke's garden there was a great and ancient cedar-tree, under which he was wont to rest on sultry days. One very warm afternoon he was sitting under this tree with two of his friends, fellow-*goshi*, chatting and drinking wine, when he felt all of a sudden very drowsy—so drowsy that he begged his friends to excuse him for taking a nap in their presence. Then he lay down at the foot of the tree, and dreamed this dream:—

He thought that as he was lying there in his garden, he saw a procession, like the train of some great daimyo descending a hill nearby, and that he got up to look at it. A very grand procession it proved to be—more imposing than anything of the kind which he had ever seen before; and it was advancing toward his dwelling. He observed in the van of it a number of young men richly appareled, who were drawing a great lacquered palace-carriage, or *gosho-guruma*, hung with bright blue silk. When the procession arrived within a short distance of the house it halted; and a richly dressed man—evidently a person of rank—advanced from it, approached Akinosuke, bowed to him profoundly, and then said:—

"Honored Sir, you see before you a *kerai* [vassal] of the Kokuo of Tokoyo.[38] My master, the King, commands me to greet you in his august name, and to place myself wholly at your

---

38   This name "Tokoyo" is indefinite. According to circumstances it may signify any unknown country—or that undiscovered country from whose bourn no traveler returns—or that Fairyland of far-eastern fable, the Realm of Horai. The term "Kokuo" means the ruler of a country—therefore a king. The original phrase, Tokoyo no Kokuo, might be rendered here as "the Ruler of Horai," or "the King of Fairyland."

disposal. He also bids me inform you that he augustly desires your presence at the palace. Be therefore pleased immediately to enter this honorable carriage, which he has sent for your conveyance."

Upon hearing these words Akinosuke wanted to make some fitting reply; but he was too much astonished and embarrassed for speech;—and in the same moment his will seemed to melt away from him, so that he could only do as the *kerai* bade him. He entered the carriage; the *kerai* took a place beside him, and made a signal; the drawers, seizing the silken ropes, turned the great vehicle southward;—and the journey began.

In a very short time, to Akinosuke's amazement, the carriage stopped in front of a huge two-storied gateway (*romon*), of a Chinese style, which he had never before seen. Here the *kerai* dismounted, saying, "I go to announce the honorable arrival,"— and he disappeared. After some little waiting, Akinosuke saw two noble-looking men, wearing robes of purple silk and high caps of the form indicating lofty rank, come from the gateway. These, after having respectfully saluted him, helped him to descend from the carriage, and led him through the great gate and across a vast garden, to the entrance of a palace whose front appeared to extend, west and east, to a distance of miles. Akinosuke was then shown into a reception-room of wonderful size and splendor. His guides conducted him to the place of honor, and respectfully seated themselves apart; while serving-maids, in costume of ceremony, brought refreshments. When Akinosuke had partaken of the refreshments, the two purple-robed attendants bowed low before him, and addressed him in the following words—each speaking alternately, according to the etiquette of courts:—

"It is now our honorable duty to inform you... as to the reason of your having been summoned hither... Our master, the King, augustly desires that you become his son-in-law;... and it is his wish and command that you shall wed this very day... the August Princess, his maiden-daughter... We shall soon conduct you to the presence-chamber... where His Augustness even now is waiting to receive you... But it will be necessary that we first invest you... with the appropriate garments of ceremony."[39]

Having thus spoken, the attendants rose together, and proceeded to an alcove containing a great chest of gold lacquer. They opened the chest, and took from it various roes and girdles of rich material, and a *kamuri*, or regal headdress. With these they attired Akinosuke as befitted a princely bridegroom; and he was then conducted to the presence-room, where he saw the Kokuo of Tokoyo seated upon the *daiza*,[40] wearing a high black cap of state, and robed in robes of yellow silk. Before the *daiza*, to left and right, a multitude of dignitaries sat in rank, motionless and splendid as images in a temple; and Akinosuke, advancing into their midst, saluted the king with the triple prostration of usage. The king greeted him with gracious words, and then said:—

"You have already been informed as to the reason of your having been summoned to Our presence. We have decided that you shall become the adopted husband of Our only daughter;— and the wedding ceremony shall now be performed."

As the king finished speaking, a sound of joyful music was heard; and a long train of beautiful court ladies advanced from behind a curtain to conduct Akinosuke to the room in which he bride awaited him.

The room was immense; but it could scarcely contain the multitude of guests assembled to witness the wedding ceremony. All bowed down before Akinosuke as he took his place, facing the King's daughter, on the kneeling-cushion prepared for him. As a maiden of heaven the bride appeared to be; and her robes

---

39   The last phrase, according to old custom, had to be uttered by both attendants at the same time. All these ceremonial observances can still be studied on the Japanese stage.

40   This was the name given to the estrade, or dais, upon which a feudal prince or ruler sat in state. The term literally signifies "great seat."

were beautiful as a summer sky. And the marriage was performed amid great rejoicing.

Afterwards the pair were conducted to a suite of apartments that had been prepared for them in another portion of the palace; and there they received the congratulations of many noble persons, and wedding gifts beyond counting.

Some days later Akinosuke was again summoned to the throne-room. On this occasion he was received even more graciously than before; and the King said to him:—

"In the southwestern part of Our dominion there is an island called Raishu. We have now appointed you Governor of that island. You will find the people loyal and docile; but their laws have not yet been brought into proper accord with the laws of Tokoyo; and their customs have not been properly regulated. We entrust you with the duty of improving their social condition as far as may be possible; and We desire that you shall rule them with kindness and wisdom. All preparations necessary for your journey to Raishu have already been made."

So Akinosuke and his bride departed from the palace of Tokoyo, accompanied to the shore by a great escort of nobles and officials; and they embarked upon a ship of state provided by the king. And with favoring winds they safety sailed to Raishu, and found the good people of that island assembled upon the beach to welcome them.

Akinosuke entered at once upon his new duties; and they did not prove to be hard. During the first three years of his governorship he was occupied chiefly with the framing and the enactment of laws; but he had wise counselors to help him, and he never found the work unpleasant. When it was all finished, he had no active duties to perform, beyond attending the rites and ceremonies ordained by ancient custom. The country was so healthy and so fertile that sickness and want were unknown; and the people were so good that no laws were ever broken. And Akinosuke dwelt and ruled in Raishu for twenty years more—making in all twenty-three years of sojourn, during which no shadow of sorrow traversed his life.

But in the twenty-fourth year of his governorship, a great misfortune came upon him; for his wife, who had borne him seven children—five boys and two girls—fell sick and died. She was buried, with high pomp, on the summit of a beautiful hill in the district of Hanryoko; and a monument, exceedingly splendid, was placed upon her grave. But Akinosuke felt such grief at her death that he no longer cared to live.

Now when the legal period of mourning was over, there came to Raishu, from the Tokoyo palace, a *shisha*, or royal messenger. The *shisha* delivered to Akinosuke a message of condolence, and then said to him:—

"These are the words which our august master, the King of Tokoyo, commands that I repeat to you: 'We will now send you back to your own people and country. As for the seven children, they are the grandsons and granddaughters of the King, and shall be fitly cared for. Do not, therefore, allow your mind to be troubled concerning them.'"

On receiving this mandate, Akinosuke submissively prepared for his departure. When all his affairs had been settled, and the ceremony of bidding farewell to his counselors and trusted officials had been concluded, he was escorted with much honor to the port. There he embarked upon the ship sent for him; and the ship sailed out into the blue sea, under the blue sky; and the shape of the island of Raishu itself turned blue, and then turned gray, and then vanished forever... And Akinosuke suddenly awoke—under the cedar-tree in his own garden!

For a moment he was stupefied and dazed. But he perceived his two friends still seated near him—drinking and chatting merrily. He stared at them in a bewildered way, and cried aloud—

"How strange!"

"Akinosuke must have been dreaming," one of them exclaimed, with a laugh. "What did you see, Akinosuke, that was strange?"

Then Akinosuke told his dream—that dream of three-and-twenty years' sojourn in the realm of Tokoyo, in the island of Raishu;—and they were astonished, because he had really slept for no more than a few minutes.

One *goshi* said:—

"Indeed, you saw strange things. We also saw something strange while you were napping. A little yellow butterfly was fluttering over your face for a moment or two; and we watched it. Then it alighted on the ground beside you, close to the tree; and almost as soon as it alighted there, a big, big ant came out of a hole and seized it and pulled it down into the hole. Just before you woke up, we saw that very butterfly come out of the hole again, and flutter over your face as before. And then it suddenly disappeared: we do not know where it went."

"Perhaps it was Akinosuke's soul," the other *goshi* said;—"certainly I thought I saw it fly into his mouth... But, even if that butterfly was Akinosuke's soul, the fact would not explain his dream."

"The ants might explain it," returned the first speaker. "Ants are queer beings—possibly goblins... Anyhow, there is a big ants' nest under that cedar-tree."...

"Let us look!" cried Akinosuke, greatly moved by this suggestion. And he went for a spade.

The ground about and beneath the cedar-tree proved to have been excavated, in a most surprising way, by a prodigious colony of ants. The ants had furthermore built inside their excavations; and their tiny constructions of straw, clay, and stems bore an odd resemblance to miniature towns. In the middle of a structure considerably larger than the rest there was a marvelous swarming of small ants around the body of one very big ant, which had yellowish wings and a long black head.

"Why, there is the King of my dream!" cried Akinosuke; "and there is the palace of Tokoyo!... How extraordinary!... Raishu ought to lie somewhere southwest of it—to the left of that big root... Yes!—here it is!... How very strange! Now I am sure that I can find the mountain of Hanryoko, and the grave of the princess."...

In the wreck of the nest he searched and searched, and at last discovered a tiny mound, on the top of which was fixed a water-worn pebble, in shape resembling a Buddhist monument. Underneath it he found—embedded in clay—the dead body of a female ant.

THE MIRROR MAIDEN

In the period of the Ashikaga Shōgunate the shrine of Ogawachi-Myōjin, at Minami-Isé, fell into decay; and the daimyō of the district, the Lord Kitahataké, found himself unable, by reason of war and other circumstances, to provide for the reparation of the building. Then the Shintō priest in charge, Matsumura Hyōgo, sought help at Kyōto from the great daimyō Hosokawa, who was known to have influence with the Shōgun. The Lord Hosokawa received the priest kindly, and promised to speak to the Shōgun about the condition of Ogawachi-Myōjin. But he said that, in any event, a grant for the restoration of the temple could not be made without due investigation and considerable delay; and he advised Matsumura to remain in the capital while the matter was being arranged. Matsumura therefore brought his family to Kyōto, and rented a house in the old Kyōgoku quarter.

This house, although handsome and spacious, had been long unoccupied. It was said to be an unlucky house. On the northeast side of it there was a well; and several former tenants had drowned themselves in that well, without any known cause. But Matsumura, being a Shintō priest, had no fear of evil spirits; and he soon made himself very comfortable in his new home.

In the summer of that year there was a great drought. For months no rain had fallen in the Five Home-Provinces; the river-beds dried up, the wells failed; and even in the capital there was a dearth of water. But the well in Matsumura's garden remained nearly full; and the water—which was very cold and clear, with a faint bluish tinge—seemed to be supplied by a spring. During the hot season many people came from all parts of the city to beg for water; and Matsumura allowed them to draw as much as they pleased. Nevertheless the supply did not appear to be diminished.

But one morning the dead body of a young servant, who had been sent from a neighboring residence to fetch water, was found floating in the well. No cause for a suicide could be imagined; and Matsumura, remembering many unpleasant stories about the well, began to suspect some invisible malevolence. He went to examine the well, with the intention of having a fence built around it; and while standing there alone he was startled by a sudden motion in the water, as of something alive. The motion soon ceased; and then he perceived, clearly reflected in the still surface, the figure of a young woman, apparently about nineteen or twenty years of age. She seemed to be occupied with her toilet: he distinctly saw her touching her lips with *béni*.[41] At first her face was visible in profile only; but presently she turned towards him and smiled. Immediately he felt a strange shock at his heart, and a dizziness came upon him like the dizziness of wine, and everything became dark, except that smiling face— white and beautiful as moonlight, and always seeming to grow more beautiful, and to be drawing him down—down—down into the darkness. But with a desperate effort he recovered his will and closed his eyes. When he opened them again, the face was gone, and the light had returned; and he found himself leaning down over the curb of the well. A moment more of that dizziness—a moment more of that dazzling lure—and he would never again have looked upon the sun...

Returning to the house, he gave orders to his people not to approach the well under any circumstances, or allow any person to draw water from it. And the next day he had a strong fence built round the well.

About a week after the fence had been built, the long drought was broken by a great rain-storm, accompanied by wind and lightning and thunder—thunder so tremendous that the whole city shook to the rolling of it, as if shaken by an earthquake. For three days and three nights the downpour and the lightnings and the thunder continued; and the Kamogawa rose as it had never risen before, carrying away many bridges. During the third night of the storm, at the Hour of the Ox, there was heard a

---

41   A kind of rouge, now used only to color the lips.

knocking at the door of the priest's dwelling, and the voice of a woman pleading for admittance. But Matsumura, warned by his experience at the well, forbade his servants to answer the appeal. He went himself to the entrance, and asked—

"Who calls?"

A feminine voice responded:—

"Pardon! it is I—Yayoi![42]... I have something to say to Matsumura Sama—something of great moment. Please open!"...

Matsumura half opened the door, very cautiously; and he saw the same beautiful face that had smiled upon him from the well. But it was not smiling now: it had a very sad look.

"Into my house you shall not come," the priest exclaimed. "You are not a human being, but a Well-Person.... Why do you thus wickedly try to delude and destroy people?"

The Well-Person made answer in a voice musical as a tinkling of jewels (*tama-wo-korogasu-koë*):—

"It is of that very matter that I want to speak.... I have never wished to injure human beings. But from ancient time a Poison-Dragon dwelt in that well. He was the Master of the Well; and because of him the well was always full. Long ago I fell into the water there, and so became subject to him; and he had power to make me lure people to death, in order that he might drink their blood. But now the Heavenly Ruler has commanded the Dragon to dwell hereafter in the lake called Torii-no-Iké, in the Province of Shinshō; and the gods have decided that he shall never be allowed to return to this city. So to-night, after he had gone away, I was able to come out, to beg for your kindly help. There is now very little water in the well, because of the Dragon's departure; and if you will order a search to be made, my body will be found there. I pray you to save my body from the well without delay; and I shall certainly return your benevolence."...

So saying, she vanished into the night.

Before dawn the tempest had passed; and when the sun arose there was no trace of cloud in the pure blue sky. Matsumura

---

42   This name, though uncommon, is still in use.

sent at an early hour for well-cleaners to search the well. Then, to everybody's surprise, the well proved to be almost dry. It was easily cleaned; and at the bottom of it were found some hair-ornaments of a very ancient fashion, and a metal mirror of curious form—but no trace of any body, animal or human.

Matusmura imagined, however, that the mirror might yield some explanation of the mystery; for every such mirror is a weird thing, having a soul of its own—and the soul of a mirror is feminine. This mirror, which seemed to be very old, was deeply crusted with scurf. But when it had been carefully cleaned, by the priest's order, it proved to be of rare and costly workmanship; and there were wonderful designs upon the back of it—also several characters. Some of the characters had become indistinguishable; but there could still be discerned part of a date, and ideographs signifying, "*third month, the third day.*" Now the third month used to be termed *Yayoi* (meaning, the Month of Increase); and the third day of the third month, which is a festival day, is still called *Yayoi-no-sekku*. Remembering that the Well-Person called herself "Yayoi," Matsumura felt almost sure that his ghostly visitant had been none other than the Soul of the Mirror.

He therefore resolved to treat the mirror with all the consideration due to a Spirit. After having caused it to be carefully repolished and resilvered, he had a case of precious wood made for it, and a particular room in the house prepared to receive it. On the evening of the same day that it had been respectfully deposited in that room, Yayoi herself unexpectedly appeared before the priest as he sat alone in his study. She looked even more lovely than before; but the light of her beauty was now soft as the light of a summer moon shining through pure white clouds. After having humbly saluted Matsumura, she said in her sweetly tinkling voice:—

"Now that you have saved me from solitude and sorrow, I have come to thank you.... I am indeed, as you supposed, the Spirit of the Mirror. It was in the time of the Emperor Saimei that I was first brought here from Kudara; and I dwelt in the august residence until the time of the Emperor Saga, when I was augustly bestowed upon the Lady Kamo, Naishinnō of the Imperial Court.[43] Thereafter I became an heirloom in the House of Fuji-wara, and so remained until the period of Hōgen, when I was dropped into the well. There I was left and forgotten during the years of the great war.[44] The Master of the Well[45] was a venomous Dragon, who used to live in a lake that once covered a great part of this district. After the lake had been filled in, by government order, in order that houses might be built upon the place of it, the Dragon took possession of the well; and when I fell into the well I became subject to him; and he compelled me to lure many people to their deaths. But the gods have banished him forever.... Now I have one more favor to beseech: I entreat that you will cause me to be offered up to the Shōgun, the Lord Yoshimasa, who by descent is related to my former possessors. Do me but this last great kindness, and it will bring you good-fortune.... But I have also to warn you of a danger. In this house, after to-morrow, you must not stay, because it will be destroyed."... And with these words of warning Yayoi disappeared.

Matsumura was able to profit by this premonition. He removed his people and his belongings to another district the next day; and almost immediately afterwards another storm arose, even

---

43   The Emperor Saimei reigned from 655 to 662; the Emperor Saga from 810 to 842. Kudara was an ancient kingdom in southwestern Korea, frequently mentioned in early Japanese history. A *Naishinn* was of Imperial blood. In the ancient court-hierarchy there were twenty-five ranks or grades of noble ladies; that of *Naishinno* was seventh in order of precedence.

44   For centuries the wives of the emperors and the ladies of the Imperial Court were chosen from the Fujiwara clan. The period called Hōgen lasted from 1156 to 1159: the war referred to is the famous war between the Taira and Minamoto clans.

45   In old-time belief every lake or spring had its invisible guardian, supposed to sometimes take the form of a serpent or dragon. The spirit of a lake or pond was commonly spoken of as *Iké-no-Mushi*, the Master of the Lake. Here we find the title "Master" given to a dragon living in a well; but the guardian of wells is really the god Suijin.

more violent than the first, causing a flood which swept away the house in which he had been residing.

Some time later, by favor of the Lord Hosokawa, Matsumura was enabled to obtain an audience of the Shōgun Yoshimasa, to whom he presented the mirror, together with a written account of its wonderful history. Then the prediction of the Spirit of the Mirror was fulfilled; for the Shōgun, greatly pleased with this strange gift, not only bestowed costly presents upon Matsumura, but also made an ample grant of money for the rebuilding of the Temple of Ogawachi-Myōjin.

THE RECONCILIATION

There was a young Samurai of Kyōto who had been reduced to poverty by the ruin of his lord, and found himself obliged to leave his home, and to take service with the Governor of a distant province. Before quitting the capital, this Samurai divorced his wife—a good and beautiful woman—under the belief that he could better obtain promotion by another alliance. He then married the daughter of a family of some distinction, and took her with him to the district whither he had been called.

But it was in the time of the thoughtlessness of youth, and the sharp experience of want, that the Samurai could not understand the worth of the affection so lightly cast away. His second marriage did not prove a happy one; the character of his new wife was hard and selfish; and he soon found every cause to think with regret of Kyōto days. Then he discovered that he still loved his first wife—loved her more than he could ever love the second; and he began to feel how unjust and how thankless he had been. Gradually his repentance deepened into a remorse that left him no peace of mind. Memories of the woman he had wronged—her gentle speech, her smiles, her dainty, pretty ways, her faultless patience—continually haunted him. Sometimes in dreams he saw her at her loom, weaving as when she toiled night and day to help him during the years of their distress: more often he saw her kneeling alone in the desolate little room where he had left her, veiling her tears with her poor worn sleeve. Even in the hours of official duty, his thoughts would wander back to her: then he would ask himself how she was living, what she was doing. Something in his heart assured him that she could not accept another husband, and that she never would refuse to pardon him. And he secretly resolved to seek her out as soon as he could return to Kyōto—then to beg her forgiveness, to take her back, to do everything that a man could do to make atonement. But the years went by.

At last the Governor's official term expired, and the Samurai was free. "Now I will go back to my dear one," he vowed to himself. "Ah, what a cruelty—what a folly to have divorced her!" He sent his second wife to her own people (she had given him no children); and hurrying to Kyōto, he went at once to seek his former companion—not allowing himself even the time to change his travelling-garb.

When he reached the street where she used to live, it was late in the night—the night of the tenth day of the ninth month;— and the city was silent as a cemetery. But a bright moon made everything visible; and he found the house without difficulty. It had a deserted look: tall weeds were growing on the roof. He knocked at the sliding-doors, and no one answered. Then, finding that the doors had not been fastened from within, he pushed them open, and entered. The front room was matless and empty: a chilly wind was blowing through crevices in the planking; and the moon shone through a ragged break in the wall of the alcove. Other rooms presented a like forlorn condition. The house, to all seeming, was unoccupied. Nevertheless, the Samurai determined to visit one other apartment at the further end of the dwelling—a very small room that had been his wife's favorite resting-place. Approaching the sliding-screen that closed it, he was startled to perceive a glow within. He pushed the screen aside, and uttered a cry of joy; for he saw her there—sewing by the light of a paper-lamp. Her eyes at the same instant met his own; and with a happy smile she greeted him—asking only:— "When did you come back to Kyōto? How did you find your way here to me, through all those black rooms?" The years had not changed her. Still she seemed as fair and young as in his fondest memory of her;—but sweeter than any memory there came to him the music of her voice, with its trembling of pleased wonder.

Then joyfully he took his place beside her, and told her all:— how deeply he repented his selfishness—how wretched he had been without her—how constantly he had regretted her—how long he had hoped and planned to make amends;—caressing her the while, and asking her forgiveness over and over again. She answered him, with loving gentleness, according to his heart's desire—entreating him to cease all self-reproach. It was wrong, she said, that he should have allowed himself to suffer on her account: she had always felt that she was not worthy to be his wife. She knew that he had separated from her, notwithstanding, only because of poverty; and while he lived with her, he had always been kind; and she had never ceased to pray for his happiness. But even if there had been a reason for speaking of amends, this honorable visit would be ample amends;—what greater happiness than thus to see him again, though it were only for a moment? "Only for a moment!" he answered, with a glad laugh—"say, rather, for the time of seven existences! My loved one, unless you forbid, I am coming back to live with you always—always—always! Nothing shall ever separate us again. Now I have means and friends: we need not fear poverty. To-morrow my goods will be brought here; and my servants will come to wait upon you; and we shall make this house beautiful.... To-night," he added, apologetically, "I came thus late—without even changing my dress—only because of the longing I had to see you, and to tell you this." She seemed greatly pleased by these words; and in her turn she told him about all that had happened in Kyōto since the time of his departure—excepting her own sorrows, of which she sweetly refused to speak. They chatted far into the night: then she conducted him to a warmer room, facing south—a room that had been their bridal chamber in former time. "Have you no one in the house to help you?" he asked, as she began to prepare the couch for him. "No," she answered, laughing cheerfully: "I could not afford a servant;—so I have been living all alone."

"You will have plenty of servants to-morrow," he said—"good servants—and everything else that you need." They lay down to rest—not to sleep: they had too much to tell each other;—and they talked of the past and the present and the future, until the dawn was gray. Then, involuntarily, the Samurai closed his eyes, and slept.

When he awoke, the daylight was streaming through the chinks of the sliding-shutters; and he found himself, to his utter amazement, lying upon the naked boards of a mouldering floor.... Had he only dreamed a dream? No: she was there;—she slept.... He bent above her—and looked—and shrieked;—for the sleeper had no face!... Before him, wrapped in its grave-sheet only, lay the corpse of a woman—a corpse so wasted that little remained save the bones, and the long black tangled hair.

Slowly—as he stood shuddering and sickening in the sun—the icy horror yielded to a despair so intolerable, a pain so atrocious, that he clutched at the mocking shadow of a doubt. Feigning ignorance of the neighborhood, he ventured to ask his way to the house in which his wife had lived.

"There is no one in that house," said the person questioned. "It used to belong to the wife of a Samurai who left the city several years ago. He divorced her in order to marry another woman before he went away; and she fretted a great deal, and so became sick. She had no relatives in Kyōto, and nobody to care for her; and she died in the autumn of the same year—on the tenth day of the ninth month...."

A PASSIONAL KARMA

One of the never-failing attractions of the Tōkyō stage is the performance, by the famous Kikugorō and his company, of the Botan-Dōrō, or "Peony-Lantern." This weird play, of which the scenes are laid in the middle of the last century, is the dramatization of a romance by the novelist Encho, written in colloquial Japanese, and purely Japanese in local color, though inspired by a Chinese tale. I went to see the play; and Kikugorō made me familiar with a new variety of the pleasure of fear. "Why not give English readers the ghostly part of the story?"—asked a friend who guides me betimes through the mazes of Eastern philosophy. "It would serve to explain some popular ideas of the supernatural which Western people know very little about. And I could help you with the translation."

I gladly accepted the suggestion; and we composed the following summary of the more extraordinary portion of Encho's romance. Here and there we found it necessary to condense the original narrative; and we tried to keep close to the text only in the conversational passages—some of which happen to possess a particular quality of psychological interest.

—This is the story of the Ghosts in the Romance of the Peony-Lantern:—

I

There once lived in the district of Ushigomé, in Yedo, a *hatamoto*[46] called Iijima Heizayémon, whose only daughter, Tsuyu, was beautiful as her name, which signifies "Morning Dew." Iijima took a second wife when his daughter was about sixteen; and,

---

46   The *hatamoto* were samurai forming the special military force of the Shogun. The name literally signifies "Banner-Supporters." These were the highest class of samurai—not only as the immediate vassals of the Shogun, but as a military aristocracy.

finding that O-Tsuyu could not be happy with her mother-in-law, he had a pretty villa built for the girl at Yanagijima, as a separate residence, and gave her an excellent maidservant, called O-Yoné, to wait upon her.

O-Tsuyu lived happily enough in her new home until one day when the family physician, Yamamoto Shijō, paid her a visit in company with a young samurai named Hagiwara Shinzaburō, who resided in the Nedzu quarter. Shinzaburō was an unusually handsome lad, and very gentle; and the two young people fell in love with each other at sight. Even before the brief visit was over, they contrived—unheard by the old doctor—to pledge themselves to each other for life. And, at parting, O-Tsuyu whispered to the youth—"*Remember! If you do not come to see me again, I shall certainly die!*"

Shinzaburō never forgot those words; and he was only too eager to see more of O-Tsuyu. But etiquette forbade him to make the visit alone: he was obliged to wait for some other chance to accompany the doctor, who had promised to take him to the villa a second time. Unfortunately the old man did not keep this promise. He had perceived the sudden affection of O-Tsuyu; and he feared that her father would hold him responsible for any serious results. Iijima Heizayémon had a reputation for cutting off heads. And the more Shijō thought about the possible consequences of his introduction of Shinzaburō at the Iijima villa, the more he became afraid. Therefore he purposely abstained from calling upon his young friend.

Months passed; and O-Tsuyu, little imagining the true cause of Shinzaburō's neglect, believed that her love had been scorned. Then she pined away, and died. Soon afterwards, the faithful servant O-Yoné also died, through grief at the loss of her mistress; and the two were buried side by side in the cemetery of Shin-Banzui-In—a temple which still stands in the neighborhood of Dango-Zaka, where the famous chrysanthemum-shows are yearly held.

II

Shinzaburō knew nothing of what had happened; but his disappointment and his anxiety had resulted in a prolonged illness. He was slowly recovering, but still very weak, when he unexpectedly received another visit from Yamamoto Shijō. The old man made a number of plausible excuses for his apparent neglect. Shinzaburō said to him:—"I have been sick ever since the beginning of spring;—even now I cannot eat anything.... Was it not rather unkind of you never to call? I thought that we were to make another visit together to the house of the Lady Iijima; and I wanted to take to her some little present as a return for our kind reception. Of course I could not go by myself."

Shijō gravely responded—"I am very sorry to tell you that the young lady is dead!"

"Dead!" repeated Shinzaburō, turning white—"did you say that she is dead?"

The doctor remained silent for a moment, as if collecting himself: then he resumed, in the quick light tone of a man resolved not to take trouble seriously:—

"My great mistake was in having introduced you to her; for it seems that she fell in love with you at once. I am afraid that you must have said something to encourage this affection—when you were in that little room together. At all events, I saw how she felt towards you; and then I became uneasy—fearing that her father might come to hear of the matter, and lay the whole blame upon me. So—to be quite frank with you—I decided that it would be better not to call upon you; and I purposely stayed away for a long time. But, only a few days ago, happening to visit Iijima's house, I heard, to my great surprise, that his daughter had died, and that her servant O-Yoné had also died. Then, remembering all that had taken place, I knew that the young lady must have died of love for you.... [Laughing] Ah, you are really a sinful fellow! Yes, you are! [Laughing] Isn't it a sin to have been born so handsome that the girls die for love of you? [Seriously] Well, we must leave the dead to the dead. It is no use to talk further about the matter;—all that you now can do for her is to repeat the Nembutsu[47].... Good-bye."

And the old man retired hastily—anxious to avoid further converse about the painful event for which he felt himself to have been unwittingly responsible.

III

Shinzaburō long remained stupefied with grief by the news of O-Tsuyu's death. But as soon as he found himself again able to think clearly, he inscribed the dead girl's name upon a mortuary tablet, and placed the tablet in the Buddhist shrine of his house, and set offerings before it, and recited prayers. Every day thereafter he presented offerings, and repeated the Nembutsu; and the memory of O-Tsuyu was never absent from his thought.

Nothing occurred to change the monotony of his solitude before the time of the Bon—the great Festival of the Dead—which begins upon the thirteenth day of the seventh month. Then he decorated his house, and prepared everything for the festival;—hanging out the lanterns that guide the returning spirits, and setting the food of ghosts on the shōryōdana, or Shelf of Souls. And on the first evening of the Bon, after sun-down, he kindled a small lamp before the tablet of O-Tsuyu, and lighted the lanterns.

The night was clear, with a great moon—and windless, and very warm. Shinzaburō sought the coolness of his veranda. Clad only in a light summer-robe, he sat there thinking, dreaming, sorrowing;—sometimes fanning himself; sometimes making a little smoke to drive the mosquitoes away. Everything was quiet. It was a lonesome neighborhood, and there were few passers-by. He could hear only the soft rushing of a neighboring stream, and the shrilling of night-insects.

---

47   The invocation *Namu Amida Butsu!* ("Hail to the Buddha Amitabha!"), repeated, as a prayer, for the sake of the dead.

But all at once this stillness was broken by a sound of women's *geta*[48] approaching—*kara-kon, kara-kon*;—and the sound drew nearer and nearer, quickly, till it reached the live-hedge surrounding the garden. Then Shinzaburō, feeling curious, stood on tiptoe, so as to look over the hedge; and he saw two women passing. One, who was carrying a beautiful lantern decorated with peony-flowers,[49] appeared to be a servant;—the other was a slender girl of about seventeen, wearing a long-sleeved robe embroidered with designs of autumn-blossoms. Almost at the same instant both women turned their faces toward Shinzaburō;—and to his utter astonishment, he recognized O-Tsuyu and her servant O-Yoné.

They stopped immediately; and the girl cried out—"Oh, how strange!... Hagiwara Sama!"

Shinzaburō simultaneously called to the maid:—"O-Yoné! Ah, you are O-Yoné!—I remember you very well."

"Hagiwara Sama!" exclaimed O-Yoné in a tone of supreme amazement. "Never could I have believed it possible!... Sir, we were told that you had died."

"How extraordinary!" cried Shinzaburō. "Why, I was told that both of you were dead!"

"Ah, what a hateful story!" returned O-Yoné. "Why repeat such unlucky words?... Who told you?"

"Please to come in," said Shinzaburō;—"here we can talk better. The garden-gate is open."

So they entered, and exchanged greeting; and when Shinzaburō had made them comfortable, he said:—

---

48   *Komageta* in the original. The *geta* is a wooden sandal, or clog, of which there are many varieties—some decidedly elegant. The *komageta*, or "pony-geta" is so-called because of the sonorous hoof-like echo which it makes on hard ground.

49   The sort of lantern here referred to is no longer made. It was totally unlike the modern domestic band-lantern, painted with the owner's crest; but it was not altogether unlike some forms of lanterns still manufactured for the Festival of the Dead, and called Bon-dōr. The flowers ornamenting it were not painted: they were artificial flowers of crepe-silk, and were attached to the top of the lantern.

"I trust that you will pardon mȳ discourtesy in not having called upon you for so long a time. But Shijō, the doctor, about a month ago, told me that you had both died."

"So it was he who told you?" exclaimed O-Yoné. "It was very wicked of him to say such a thing. Well, it was also Shijō who told us that you were dead. I think that he wanted to deceive you—which was not a difficult thing to do, because you are so confiding and trustful. Possibly my mistress betrayed her liking for you in some words which found their way to her father's ears; and, in that case, O-Kuni—the new wife—might have planned to make the doctor tell you that we were dead, so as to bring about a separation. Anyhow, when my mistress heard that you had died, she wanted to cut off her hair immediately, and to become a nun. But I was able to prevent her from cutting off her hair; and I persuaded her at last to become a nun only in her heart. Afterwards her father wished her to marry a certain young man; and she refused. Then there was a great deal of trouble—chiefly caused by O-Kuni;—and we went away from the villa, and found a very small house in Yanaka-no-Sasaki. There we are now just barely able to live, by doing a little private work.... My mistress has been constantly repeating the Nembutsu for your sake. To-day, being the first day of the Bon, we went to visit the temples; and we were on our way home—thus late— when this strange meeting happened."

"Oh, how extraordinary!" cried Shinzaburō. "Can it be true?— or is it only a dream? Here I, too, have been constantly reciting the Nembutsu before a tablet with her name upon it! Look!" And he showed them O-Tsuyu's tablet in its place upon the Shelf of Souls.

"We are more than grateful for your kind remembrance," returned O-Yoné, smiling.... "Now as for my mistress,"—she continued, turning towards O-Tsuyu, who had all the while remained demure and silent, half-hiding her face with her sleeve—"as for my mistress, she actually says that she would not mind being disowned by her father for the time of seven exist-

ences,[50] or even being killed by him, for your sake! Come! will
you not allow her to stay here to-night?"

Shinzaburō turned pale for joy. He answered in a voice trembling with emotion:—"Please remain; but do not speak
loud—because there is a troublesome fellow living close by—a
ninsomi[51] called Hakuōdō Yusai, who tells people's fortunes by
looking at their faces. He is inclined to be curious; and it is better
that he should not know."

The two women remained that night in the house of the
young samurai, and returned to their own home a little before
daybreak. And after that night they came every night for seven
nights—whether the weather were foul or fair—always at the
same hour. And Shinzaburō became more and more attached to
the girl; and the twain were fettered, each to each, by that bond
of illusion which is stronger than bands of iron.

IV

Now there was a man called Tomozō, who lived in a small cottage
adjoining Shinzaburō's residence, Tomozō and his wife O-Miné
were both employed by Shinzaburō as servants. Both seemed to
be devoted to their young master; and by his help they were
able to live in comparative comfort.

One night, at a very late hour, Tomozō heard the voice of a
woman in his master's apartment; and this made him uneasy. He
feared that Shinzaburō, being very gentle and affectionate, might

---

50   "For the time of seven existences,"—that is to say, for the time
of seven successive lives. In Japanese drama and romance it is not
uncommon to represent a father as disowning his child "for the time
of seven lives." Such a disowning is called shichi-shō madé no mandō,
a disinheritance for seven lives—signifying that in six future lives after
the present the erring son or daughter will continue to feel the parental
displeasure.

51   The profession is not yet extinct. The *ninsomi* uses a kind of
magnifying glass (or magnifying-mirror sometimes) called tengankyō
or *ninsomégané*.

be made the dupe of some cunning wanton—in which event the domestics would be the first to suffer. He therefore resolved to watch; and on the following night he stole on tiptoe to Shinzaburō's dwelling, and looked through a chink in one of the sliding shutters. By the glow of a night-lantern within the sleeping-room, he was able to perceive that his master and a strange woman were talking together under the mosquito-net. At first he could not see the woman distinctly. Her back was turned to him;—he only observed that she was very slim, and that she appeared to be very young—judging from the fashion of her dress and hair.[52] Putting his ear to the chink, he could hear the conversation plainly. The woman said:—

"And if I should be disowned by my father, would you then let me come and live with you?"

Shinzaburō answered:—

"Most assuredly I would—nay, I should be glad of the chance. But there is no reason to fear that you will ever be disowned by your father; for you are his only daughter, and he loves you very much. What I do fear is that some day we shall be cruelly separated."

She responded softly:—

"Never, never could I even think of accepting any other man for my husband. Even if our secret were to become known, and my father were to kill me for what I have done, still—after death itself—I could never cease to think of you. And I am now quite sure that you yourself would not be able to live very long without me."... Then clinging closely to him, with her lips at his neck, she caressed him; and he returned her caresses.

Tomozō wondered as he listened—because the language of the woman was not the language of a common woman, but the language of a lady of rank.[53] Then he determined at all hazards

---

52   The color and form of the dress, and the style of wearing the hair, are by Japanese custom regulated according to the age of the woman.

53   The forms of speech used by the samurai, and other superior

to get one glimpse of her face; and he crept round the house, backwards and forwards, peering through every crack and chink. And at last he was able to see;—but therewith an icy trembling seized him; and the hair of his head stood up.

For the face was the face of a woman long dead—and the fingers caressing were fingers of naked bone—and of the body below the waist there was not anything: it melted off into thinnest trailing shadow. Where the eyes of the lover deluded saw youth and grace and beauty, there appeared to the eyes of the watcher horror only, and the emptiness of death. Simultaneously another woman's figure, and a weirder, rose up from within the chamber, and swiftly made toward the watcher, as if discerning his presence. Then, in uttermost terror, he fled to the dwelling of Hakuōdō Yusai, and, knocking frantically at the doors, succeeded in arousing him.

V

Hakuōdō Yusai, the *ninsomi*, was a very old man; but in his time he had traveled much, and he had heard and seen so many things that he could not be easily surprised. Yet the story of the terrified Tomozō both alarmed and amazed him. He had read in ancient Chinese books of love between the living and the dead; but he had never believed it possible. Now, however, he felt convinced that the statement of Tomozō was not a falsehood, and that something very strange was really going on in the house of Hagiwara. Should the truth prove to be what Tomozō imagined, then the young samurai was a doomed man.

"If the woman be a ghost,"—said Yusai to the frightened servant, "—if the woman be a ghost, your master must die very soon—unless something extraordinary can be done to save him. And if the woman be a ghost, the signs of death will appear upon his face. For the spirit of the living is yōki, and pure;—the

---

classes, differed considerably from those of the popular idiom; but these differences could not be effectively rendered into English.

spirit of the dead is *inki*, and unclean: the one is Positive, the other Negative. He whose bride is a ghost cannot live. Even though in his blood there existed the force of a life of one hundred years, that force must quickly perish…. Still, I shall do all that I can to save Hagiwara Sama. And in the meantime, Tomozō, say nothing to any other person—not even to your wife—about this matter. At sunrise I shall call upon your master."

VI

When questioned next morning by Yusai, Shinzaburō at first attempted to deny that any women had been visiting the house; but finding this artless policy of no avail, and perceiving that the old man's purpose was altogether unselfish, he was finally persuaded to acknowledge what had really occurred, and to give his reasons for wishing to keep the matter a secret. As for the lady Iijima, he intended, he said, to make her his wife as soon as possible.

"Oh, madness!" cried Yusai—losing all patience in the intensity of his alarm. "Know, sir, that the people who have been coming here, night after night, are dead! Some frightful delusion is upon you!… Why, the simple fact that you long supposed O-Tsuyu to be dead, and repeated the Nembutsu for her, and made offerings before her tablet, is itself the proof!… The lips of the dead have touched you!—the hands of the dead have caressed you!… Even at this moment I see in your face the signs of death—and you will not believe!… Listen to me now, sir—I beg of you—if you wish to save yourself: otherwise you have less than twenty days to live. They told you—those people—that they were residing in the district of Shitaya, in Yanaka-no-Sasaki. Did you ever visit them at that place? No!—of course you did not! Then go to-day— as soon as you can—to Yanaka-no-Sasaki, and try to find their home!…"

And having uttered this counsel with the most vehement earnestness, Hakuōdō Yusai abruptly took his departure.

Shinzaburō, startled though not convinced, resolved after a moment's reflection to follow the advice of the *ninsomi*, and to go to Shitaya. It was yet early in the morning when he reached the quarter of Yanaka-no-Sasaki, and began his search for the dwelling of O-Tsuyu. He went through every street and side-street, read all the names inscribed at the various entrances, and made inquiries whenever an opportunity presented itself. But he could not find anything resembling the little house mentioned by O-Yone; and none of the people whom he questioned knew of any house in the quarter inhabited by two single women. Feeling at last certain that further research would be useless, he turned homeward by the shortest way, which happened to lead through the grounds of the temple Shin-Banzui-In.

Suddenly his attention was attracted by two new tombs, placed side by side, at the rear of the temple. One was a common tomb, such as might have been erected for a person of humble rank: the other was a large and handsome monument; and hanging before it was a beautiful peony-lantern, which had probably been left there at the time of the Festival of the Dead. Shinzaburō remembered that the peony-lantern carried by O-Yoné was exactly similar; and the coincidence impressed him as strange. He looked again at the tombs; but the tombs explained nothing. Neither bore any personal name—only the Buddhist kaimyō, or posthumous appellation. Then he determined to seek information at the temple. An acolyte stated, in reply to his questions, that the large tomb had been recently erected for the daughter of Iijima Heizayémon, the *hatamoto* of Ushigomé; and that the small tomb next to it was that of her servant O-Yoné, who had died of grief soon after the young lady's funeral.

Immediately to Shinzaburō's memory there recurred, with another and sinister meaning, the words of O-Yoné:—"We went away, and found a very small house in Yanaka-no-Sasaki. There we are now just barely able to live—by doing a little private work...." Here was indeed the very small house—and in Yanaka-no-Sasaki. But the little private work...?

Terror-stricken, the samurai hastened with all speed to the house of Yusai, and begged for his counsel and assistance. But Yusai declared himself unable to be of any aid in such a case. All that he could do was to send Shinzaburō to the high-priest Ryōseki, of Shin-Banzui-In, with a letter praying for immediate religious help.

VII

The high-priest Ryōseki was a learned and a holy man. By spiritual vision he was able to know the secret of any sorrow, and the nature of the karma that had caused it. He heard unmoved the story of Shinzaburō, and said to him:—

"A very great danger now threatens you, because of an error committed in one of your former states of existence. The karma that binds you to the dead is very strong; but if I tried to explain its character, you would not be able to understand. I shall therefore tell you only this—that the dead person has no desire to injure you out of hate, feels no enmity towards you: she is influenced, on the contrary, by the most passionate affection for you. Probably the girl has been in love with you from a time long preceding your present life—from a time of not less than three or four past existences; and it would seem that, although necessarily changing her form and condition at each succeeding birth, she has not been able to cease from following after you. Therefore it will not be an easy thing to escape from her influence…. But now I am going to lend you this powerful *mamori*.[54] It is a pure gold image of that Buddha called

---

54   The Japanese word *mamori* has significations at least as numerous as those attaching to our own term "amulet." It would be impossible, in a mere footnote, even to suggest the variety of Japanese religious objects to which the name is given. In this instance, the *mamori* is a very small image, probably enclosed in a miniature shrine of lacquer-work or metal, over which a silk cover is drawn. Such little images were often worn by samurai on the person. I was recently shown a miniature figure of Kwannon, in an iron case, which had been carried by an officer through the Satsuma war. He observed, with good

the Sea-Sounding Tathāgata—Kai-On-Nyōrai—because his preaching of the Law sounds through the world like the sound of the sea. And this little image is especially a shiryō-yoké,[55]—which protects the living from the dead. This you must wear, in its covering, next to your body—under the girdle.... Besides, I shall presently perform in the temple, a *Segaki*-service[56] for the repose of the troubled spirit....And here is a holy sutra, called Ubō-Darani-Kyō, or "Treasure-Raining Sutra":[57] you must be careful to recite it every night in your house—without fail.... Furthermore I shall give you this package of *o-fuda*;[58]—you must paste one of them over every opening of your house—no matter how small. If you do this, the power of the holy texts will prevent the dead from entering. But—whatever may happen—do not fail to recite the sutra."

---

reason, that it had probably saved his life; for it had stopped a bullet of which the dent was plainly visible.

55   From shiryō, a ghost, and *yokeru*, to exclude. The Japanese have two kinds of ghosts proper in their folklore: the spirits of the dead, shiryō; and the spirits of the living, ikiryō. A house or a person may be haunted by an ikiryō as well as by a shiryō.

56   A special service—accompanying offerings of food, etc., to those dead having no living relatives or friends to care for them—is thus termed. In this case, however, the service would be of a particular and exceptional kind.

57   The name would be more correctly written Ubō-Darani-Kyō. It is the Japanese pronunciation of the title of a very short sutra translated out of Sanscrit into Chinese by the Indian priest Amoghavajra, probably during the eighth century. The Chinese text contains transliterations of some mysterious Sanscrit words—apparently talismanic words—like those to be seen in Kern's translation of the Saddharma-Pundarika, ch. xxvi.

58   *O-fuda* is the general name given to religious texts used as charms or talismans. They are sometimes stamped or burned upon wood, but more commonly written or printed upon narrow strips of paper. *O-fuda* are pasted above house-entrances, on the walls of rooms, upon tablets placed in household shrines, etc. Some kinds are worn about the person;—others are made into pellets, and swallowed as spiritual medicine. The text of the larger *o-fuda* is often accompanied by curious pictures or symbolic illustrations.

Shinzaburō humbly thanked the high-priest; and then, taking with him the image, the sutra, and the bundle of sacred texts, he made all haste to reach his home before the hour of sunset.

VIII

With Yusai's advice and help, Shinzaburō was able before dark to fix the holy texts over all the apertures of his dwelling. Then the *ninsomi* returned to his own house—leaving the youth alone. Night came, warm and clear. Shinzaburō made fast the doors, bound the precious amulet about his waist, entered his mosquito-net, and by the glow of a night-lantern began to recite the Ubō-Darani-Kyō. For a long time he chanted the words, comprehending little of their meaning;—then he tried to obtain some rest. But his mind was still too much disturbed by the strange events of the day. Midnight passed; and no sleep came to him. At last he heard the boom of the great temple-bell of Dentsu-In announcing the eighth hour.[59]

It ceased; and Shinzaburō suddenly heard the sound of *geta* approaching from the old direction—but this time more slowly: *karan-koron, karan-koron!* At once a cold sweat broke over his forehead. Opening the sutra hastily, with trembling hand, he began again to recite it aloud. The steps came nearer and nearer—reached the live hedge—stopped! Then, strange to say, Shinzaburō felt unable to remain under his mosquito-net: something stronger even than his fear impelled him to look; and, instead of continuing to recite the Ubō-Darani-Kyō, he foolishly approached the

---

59   According to the old Japanese way of counting time, this *yatsu-doki* or eighth hour was the same as our two o'clock in the morning. Each Japanese hour was equal to two European hours, so that there were only six hours instead of our twelve; and these six hours were counted backwards in the order—9, 8, 7, 6, 5, 4. Thus the ninth hour corresponded to our midday, or midnight; half-past nine to our one o'clock; eight to our two o'clock. Two o'clock in the morning, also called "the Hour of the Ox," was the Japanese hour of ghosts and goblins.

shutters, and through a chink peered out into the night. Before the house he saw O-Tsuyu standing, and O-Yoné with the peony-lantern; and both of them were gazing at the Buddhist texts pasted above the entrance. Never before—not even in what time she lived—had O-Tsuyu appeared so beautiful; and Shinzaburō felt his heart drawn towards her with a power almost resistless. But the terror of death and the terror of the unknown restrained; and there went on within him such a struggle between his love and his fear that he became as one suffering in the body the pains of the Shō-netsu hell.[60]

Presently he heard the voice of the maid-servant, saying:—

"My dear mistress, there is no way to enter. The heart of Hagiwara Sama must have changed. For the promise that he made last night has been broken; and the doors have been made fast to keep us out.... We cannot go in to-night.... It will be wiser for you to make up your mind not to think any more about him, because his feeling towards you has certainly changed. It is evident that he does not want to see you. So it will be better not to give yourself any more trouble for the sake of a man whose heart is so unkind."

But the girl answered, weeping:—

"Oh, to think that this could happen after the pledges which we made to each other!... Often I was told that the heart of a man changes as quickly as the sky of autumn;—yet surely the heart of Hagiwara Sama cannot be so cruel that he should really intend to exclude me in this way!... Dear Yoné, please find some means of taking me to him.... Unless you do, I will never, never go home again."

Thus she continued to plead, veiling her face with her long sleeves—and very beautiful she looked, and very touching; but the fear of death was strong upon her lover.

O-Yoné at last made answer—"My dear young lady, why will

---

60   En-netsu or Shō-netsu (Sanscrit "Tapana") is the sixth of the Eight Hot Hells of Japanese Buddhism. One day of life in this hell is equal in duration to thousands (some say millions) of human years.

you trouble your mind about a man who seems to be so cruel?…
Well, let us see if there be no way to enter at the back of the
house: come with me!"

And taking O-Tsuyu by the hand, she led her away toward
the rear of the dwelling; and there the two disappeared as
suddenly as the light disappears when the flame of a lamp is
blown out.

IX

Night after night the shadows came at the Hour of the Ox; and
nightly Shinzaburō heard the weeping of O-Tsuyu. Yet he believed
himself saved—little imagining that his doom had already been
decided by the character of his dependents.

Tomozō had promised Yusai never to speak to any other
person—not even to O-Miné—of the strange events that were
taking place. But Tomozō was not long suffered by the haunters
to rest in peace. Night after night O-Yoné entered into his
dwelling, and roused him from his sleep, and asked him to remove
the *o-fuda* placed over one very small window at the back of
his master's house. And Tomozō, out of fear, as often promised
her to take away the *o-fuda* before the next sundown; but never
by day could he make up his mind to remove it—believing that
evil was intended to Shinzaburō. At last, in a night of storm,
O-Yoné startled him from slumber with a cry of reproach, and
stooped above his pillow, and said to him: "Have a care how you
trifle with us! If, by to-morrow night, you do not take away that
text, you shall learn how I can hate!" And she made her face so
frightful as she spoke that Tomozō nearly died of terror.

O-Miné, the wife of Tomozō, had never till then known of
these visits: even to her husband they had seemed like bad
dreams. But on this particular night it chanced that, waking
suddenly, she heard the voice of a woman talking to Tomozō.
Almost in the same moment the talking ceased; and when O-Miné
looked about her, she saw, by the light of the night-lamp, only

her husband—shuddering and white with fear. The stranger was gone; the doors were fast: it seemed impossible that anybody could have entered. Nevertheless the jealousy of the wife had been aroused; and she began to chide and to question Tomozō in such a manner that he thought himself obliged to betray the secret, and to explain the terrible dilemma in which he had been placed.

Then the passion of O-Miné yielded to wonder and alarm; but she was a subtle woman, and she devised immediately a plan to save her husband by the sacrifice of her master. And she gave Tomozō a cunning counsel—telling him to make conditions with the dead.

They came again on the following night at the Hour of the Ox; and O-Miné hid herself on hearing the sound of their coming—*karan-koron, karan-koron!* But Tomozō went out to meet them in the dark, and even found courage to say to them what his wife had told him to say:—

"It is true that I deserve your blame;—but I had no wish to cause you anger. The reason that the *o-fuda* has not been taken away is that my wife and I are able to live only by the help of Hagiwara Sama, and that we cannot expose him to any danger without bringing misfortune upon ourselves. But if we could obtain the sum of a hundred *ryō* in gold, we should be able to please you, because we should then need no help from anybody. Therefore if you will give us a hundred *ryō*, I can take the *o-fuda* away without being afraid of losing our only means of support."

When he had uttered these words, O-Yoné and O-Tsuyu looked at each other in silence for a moment. Then O-Yoné said:—

"Mistress, I told you that it was not right to trouble this man,—as we have no just cause of ill will against him. But it is certainly useless to fret yourself about Hagiwara Sama, because his heart has changed towards you. Now once again, my dear young lady, let me beg you not to think any more about him!"

But O-Tsuyu, weeping, made answer:—

"Dear Yoné, whatever may happen, I cannot possibly keep myself from thinking about him! You know that you can get a hundred *ryō* to have the *o-fuda* taken off.... Only once more, I pray, dear Yoné!—only once more bring me face to face with Hagiwara Sama,—I beseech you!" And hiding her face with her sleeve, she thus continued to plead.

"Oh! why will you ask me to do these things?" responded O-Yoné. "You know very well that I have no money. But since you will persist in this whim of yours, in spite of all that I can say, I suppose that I must try to find the money somehow, and to bring it here to-morrow night...." Then, turning to the faithless Tomozō, she said:—"Tomozō, I must tell you that Hagiwara Sama now wears upon his body a *mamori* called by the name of Kai-On-Nyōrai, and that so long as he wears it we cannot approach him. So you will have to get that *mamori* away from him, by some means or other, as well as to remove the *o-fuda*."

Tomozō feebly made answer:—

"That also I can do, if you will promise to bring me the hundred *ryō*."

"Well, mistress," said O-Yoné, "you will wait—will you not—until to-morrow night?"

"Oh, dear Yoné!" sobbed the other—"have we to go back to-night again without seeing Hagiwara Sama? Ah! it is cruel!"

And the shadow of the mistress, weeping, was led away by the shadow of the maid.

X

Another day went, and another night came, and the dead came with it. But this time no lamentation was heard without the house of Hagiwara; for the faithless servant found his reward at the Hour of the Ox, and removed the *o-fuda*. Moreover he had been able, while his master was at the bath, to steal from its case the golden *mamori*, and to substitute for it an image of copper; and he had buried the Kai-On-Nyōrai in a desolate field. So the visitants found nothing to oppose their entering. Veiling their faces with their sleeves they rose and passed, like a streaming of vapor, into the little window from over which the holy text had been torn away. But what happened thereafter within the house Tomozō never knew.

The sun was high before he ventured again to approach his master's dwelling, and to knock upon the sliding-doors. For the first time in years he obtained no response; and the silence made him afraid. Repeatedly he called, and received no answer. Then, aided by O-Miné, he succeeded in effecting an entrance and making his way alone to the sleeping-room, where he called again in vain. He rolled back the rumbling shutters to admit the light; but still within the house there was no stir. At last he dared to lift a corner of the mosquito-net. But no sooner had he looked beneath than he fled from the house, with a cry of horror.

Shinzaburō was dead—hideously dead;—and his face was the face of a man who had died in the uttermost agony of fear;—and lying beside him in the bed were the bones of a woman! And the bones of the arms, and the bones of the hands, clung fast about his neck.

XI

Hakuōdō Yusai, the fortune-teller, went to view the corpse at the prayer of the faithless Tomozō. The old man was terrified and astonished at the spectacle, but looked about him with a keen eye. He soon perceived that the *o-fuda* had been taken from the little window at the back of the house; and on searching the body of Shinzaburō, he discovered that the golden *mamori* had been taken from its wrapping, and a copper image of Fudō put in place of it. He suspected Tomozō of the theft; but the whole occurrence was so very extraordinary that he thought it prudent to consult with the priest Ryōseki before taking further action. Therefore, after having made a careful examination of the premises, he betook himself to the temple Shin-Banzui-In, as quickly as his aged limbs could bear him.

Ryōseki, without waiting to hear the purpose of the old man's visit, at once invited him into a private apartment.

"You know that you are always welcome here," said Ryōseki. "Please seat yourself at ease.... Well, I am sorry to tell you that Hagiwara Sama is dead."

Yusai wonderingly exclaimed:—"Yes, he is dead;—but how did you learn of it?"

The priest responded:—

"Hagiwara Sama was suffering from the results of an evil karma; and his attendant was a bad man. What happened to Hagiwara Sama was unavoidable;—his destiny had been determined from a time long before his last birth. It will be better for you not to let your mind be troubled by this event."

Yusai said:—

"I have heard that a priest of pure life may gain power to see into the future for a hundred years; but truly this is the first time in my existence that I have had proof of such power.... Still, there is another matter about which I am very anxious...."

"You mean," interrupted Ryōseki, "the stealing of the holy *mamori*, the Kai-On-Nyōrai. But you must not give yourself any concern about that. The image has been buried in a field; and it will be found there and returned to me during the eighth month of the coming year. So please do not be anxious about it."

More and more amazed, the old *ninsomi* ventured to observe:—

"I have studied the In-Yō,[61] and the science of divination; and I make my living by telling people's fortunes;—but I cannot possibly understand how you know these things."

Ryōseki answered gravely:—

"Never mind how I happen to know them.... I now want to

---

61   The Male and Female principles of the universe, the Active and Passive forces of Nature. Yusai refers here to the old Chinese nature-philosophy—better known to Western readers by the name FENG-SHUI.

speak to you about Hagiwara's funeral. The House of Hagiwara has its own family-cemetery, of course; but to bury him there would not be proper. He must be buried beside O-Tsuyu, the Lady Iijima; for his karma-relation to her was a very deep one. And it is but right that you should erect a tomb for him at your own cost, because you have been indebted to him for many favors."

Thus it came to pass that Shinzaburō was buried beside O-Tsuyu, in the cemetery of Shin-Banzui-In, in Yanaka-no-Sasaki.

—Here ends the story of the Ghosts in the Romance of the Peony-Lantern.—

My friend asked me whether the story had interested me; and I answered by telling him that I wanted to go to the cemetery of Shin-Banzui-In—so as to realize more definitely the local color of the author's studies.

"I shall go with you at once," he said. "But what did you think of the personages?"

"To Western thinking," I made answer, "Shinzaburō is a despicable creature. I have been mentally comparing him with the true lovers of our old ballad-literature. They were only too glad to follow a dead sweetheart into the grave; and nevertheless, being Christians, they believed that they had only one human life to enjoy in this world. But Shinzaburō was a Buddhist—with a million lives behind him and a million lives before him; and he was too selfish to give up even one miserable existence for the sake of the girl that came back to him from the dead. Then he was even more cowardly than selfish. Although a samurai by birth and training, he had to beg a priest to save him from ghosts. In every way he proved himself contemptible; and O-Tsuyu did quite right in choking him to death."

"From the Japanese point of view, likewise," my friend responded, "Shinzaburō is rather contemptible. But the use of this weak character helped the author to develop incidents that could not otherwise, perhaps, have been so effectively managed. To my thinking, the only attractive character in the story is that of O-Yoné: type of the old-time loyal and loving servant—intelligent, shrewd, full of resource—faithful not only unto death, but beyond death…. Well, let us go to Shin-Banzui-In."

We found the temple uninteresting, and the cemetery an abomination of desolation. Spaces once occupied by graves had been turned into potato-patches. Between were tombs leaning at all angles out of the perpendicular, tablets made illegible by scurf, empty pedestals, shattered water-tanks, and statues of Buddhas without heads or hands. Recent rains had soaked the black soil—leaving here and there small pools of slime about which swarms of tiny frogs were hopping. Everything—excepting the potato-patches—seemed to have been neglected for years. In a shed just within the gate, we observed a woman cooking; and my companion presumed to ask her if she knew anything about the tombs described in the Romance of the Peony-Lantern.

"Ah! the tombs of O-Tsuyu and O-Yoné?" she responded, smiling;—"you will find them near the end of the first row at the back of the temple—next to the statue of Jizō."

Surprises of this kind I had met with elsewhere in Japan.

We picked our way between the rain-pools and between the green ridges of young potatoes—whose roots were doubtless feeding on the substance of many another O-Tsuyu and O-Yoné;—and we reached at last two lichen-eaten tombs of which the inscriptions seemed almost obliterated. Beside the larger tomb was a statue of Jizō, with a broken nose.

"The characters are not easy to make out," said my friend—"but wait!"…. He drew from his sleeve a sheet of soft white paper, laid it over the inscription, and began to rub the paper with a lump of clay. As he did so, the characters appeared in white on the blackened surface.

"'*Eleventh day, third month—Rat, Elder Brother, Fire—Sixth year of Horeki* [A. D. 1756].'…. This would seem to be the grave of some innkeeper of Nedzu, named Kichibei. Let us see what is on the other monument."

With a fresh sheet of paper he presently brought out the text of a kaimyō, and read—

"'En-myō-In, Hō-yō-I-tei-ken-shi, Hō-ni':—'Nun-of-the-Law, Illustrious, Pure-of-heart-and-will, Famed-in-the-Law—inhabiting the Mansion-of-the-Preaching-of-Wonder.'.... The grave of some Buddhist nun."

"What utter humbug!" I exclaimed. "That woman was only making fun of us."

"Now," my friend protested, "you are unjust to the woman! You came here because you wanted a sensation; and she tried her very best to please you. You did not suppose that ghost-story was true, did you?"

THE SCREEN-MAIDEN

S ays the old Japanese author, Hakubai-En Rosui:—[62]

"In Chinese and in Japanese books there are related many stories—both of ancient and of modern times—about pictures that were so beautiful as to exercise a magical influence upon the beholder. And concerning such beautiful pictures—whether pictures of flowers or of birds or of people, painted by famous artists—it is further told that the shapes of the creatures or the persons, therein depicted, would separate themselves from the paper or the silk upon which they had been painted, and would perform various acts;—so that they became, by their own will, really alive. We shall not now repeat any of the stories of this class which have been known to everybody from ancient times. But even in modern times the fame of the pictures painted by Hishigawa Kichibei—'Hishigawa's Portraits'—has become widespread in the land."

He then proceeds to relate the following story about one of the so-called portraits:—

There was a young scholar of Kyōto whose name was Tokkei. He used to live in the street called Muromachi. One evening, while on his way home after a visit, his attention was attracted by an old single-leaf screen (*tsuitaté*), exposed for sale before the shop of a dealer in second-hand goods. It was only a paper-covered screen; but there was painted upon it the full-length figure of a girl which caught the young man's fancy. The price asked was very small: Tokkei bought the screen, and took it home with him.

---

62   He died in the eighteenth year of Kyōhō (1733). The painter to whom he refers—better known to collectors as Hishigawa Kichibei Moronobu—flourished during the latter part of the seventeenth century. Beginning his career as a dyer's apprentice, he won his reputation as an artist about 1680, when he may be said to have founded the *Ukiyo-yé* school of illustration. Hishigawa was especially a delineator of what are called *fūryū*, ("elegant manners")—the aspects of life among the upper classes of society.

When he looked again at the screen, in the solitude of his own room, the picture seemed to him much more beautiful than before. Apparently it was a real likeness—the portrait of a girl fifteen or sixteen years old; and every little detail in the painting of the hair, eyes, eyelashes, mouth, had been executed with a delicacy and a truth beyond praise. The *manajiri*[63] seemed "like a lotos-blossom courting favor"; the lips were "like the smile of a red flower"; the whole young face was inexpressibly sweet. If the real girl so portrayed had been equally lovely, no man could have looked upon her without losing his heart. And Tokkei believed that she must have been thus lovely;—for the figure seemed alive—ready to reply to anybody who might speak to it.

Gradually, as he continued to gaze at the picture, he felt himself bewitched by the charm of it. "Can there really have been in this world," he murmured to himself, "so delicious a creature? How gladly would I give my life—nay, a thousand years of life!—to hold her in my arms even for a moment!" (The Japanese author says "for a few seconds.") In short, he became enamored of the picture—so much enamored of it as to feel that he never could love any woman except the person whom it represented. Yet that person, if still alive, could no longer resemble the painting: perhaps she had been buried long before he was born!

Day by day, nevertheless, this hopeless passion grew upon him. He could not eat; he could not sleep: neither could he occupy his mind with those studies which had formerly delighted him. He would sit for hours before the picture, talking to it—neglecting or forgetting everything else. And at last he fell sick—so sick that he believed himself going to die.

Now among the friends of Tokkei there was one venerable scholar who knew many strange things about old pictures and

---

63   Also written *méjiri*—the exterior canthus of the eye. The Japanese (like the old Greek and the old Arabian poets) have many curious dainty words and similes to express particular beauties of the hair, eyes, eyelids, lips, fingers, etc.

about young hearts. This aged scholar, hearing of Tokkei's illness, came to visit him, and saw the screen, and understood what had happened. Then Tokkei, being questioned, confessed everything to his friend, and declared:—"If I cannot find such a woman, I shall die."

The old man said:—

"That picture was painted by Hishigawa Kichibei—painted from life. The person whom it represented is not now in the world. But it is said that Hishigawa Kichibei painted her mind as well as her form, and that her spirit lives in the picture. So I think that you can win her."

Tokkei half rose from his bed, and stared eagerly at the speaker.

"You must give her a name," the old man continued;—"and you must sit before her picture every day, and keep your thoughts constantly fixed upon her, and call her gently by the name which you have given her, *until she answers you*...."

"Answers me!" exclaimed the lover, in breathless amazement.

"Oh, yes," the adviser responded, "she will certainly answer you. But you must be ready, when she answers you, to present her with what I am going to tell you...."

"I will give her my life!" cried Tokkei.

"No," said the old man;—"you will present her with a cup of wine that has been bought at one hundred different wine-shops. Then she will come out of the screen to accept the wine. After that, probably she herself will tell you what to do."

With these words the old man went away. His advice aroused Tokkei from despair. At once he seated himself before the picture, and called it by the name of a girl—(what name the Japanese narrator has forgotten to tell us)—over and over again, very tenderly. That day it made no answer, nor the next day, nor the next. But Tokkei did not lose faith or patience; and after many days it suddenly one evening answered to its name—

"*Hai!*" (Yes.)

Then quickly, quickly, some of the wine from a hundred different wine-shops was poured out, and reverentially presented in a little cup. And the girl stepped from the screen, and walked upon the matting of the room, and knelt to take the cup from Tokkei's hand—asking, with a delicious smile:—

"How could you love me so much?"

Says the Japanese narrator: "She was much more beautiful than the picture—beautiful to the tips of her finger-nails—beautiful also in heart and temper—lovelier than anybody else in the world." What answer Tokkei made to her question is not recorded: it will have to be imagined.

"But will you not soon get tired of me?" she asked.

"Never while I live!" he protested.

"And after—?" she persisted;—for the Japanese bride is not satisfied with love for one life-time only.

"Let us pledge ourselves to each other," he entreated, "for the time of seven existences."

"If you are ever unkind to me," she said, "I will go back to the screen."

They pledged each other. I suppose that Tokkei was a good boy—for his bride never returned to the screen. The space that she had occupied upon it remained a blank.

Exclaims the Japanese author—

"How very seldom do such things happen in this world!"

THE STORY OF ITŌ NORISUKÉ

In the town of Uji, in the province of Yamashiro, there lived, about six hundred years ago, a young samurai named It Tatéwaki Norisuké, whose ancestors were of the Heiké clan. Itō was of handsome person and amiable character, a good scholar and apt at arms. But his family were poor; and he had no patron among the military nobility—so that his prospects were small. He lived in a very quiet way, devoting himself to the study of literature, and having (says the Japanese story-teller) "only the Moon and the Wind for friends."

One autumn evening, as he was taking a solitary walk in the neighborhood of the hill called Kotobikiyama, he happened to overtake a young girl who was following the same path. She was richly dressed, and seemed to be about eleven or twelve years old. Itō greeted her, and said, "The sun will soon be setting, damsel, and this is rather a lonesome place. May I ask if you have lost your way?" She looked up at him with a bright smile, and answered deprecatingly: "Nay! I am a *miya-dzukai*,[64] serving in this neighborhood; and I have only a little way to go."

By her use of the term *miya-dzukai*, Itō knew that the girl must be in the service of persons of rank; and her statement surprised him, because he had never heard of any family of distinction residing in that vicinity. But he only said: "I am returning to Uji, where my home is. Perhaps you will allow me to accompany you on the way, as this is a very lonesome place." She thanked him gracefully, seeming pleased by his offer; and they walked on together, chatting as they went. She talked about the weather, the flowers, the butterflies, and the birds; about a visit that she had once made to Uji, about the famous sights of the capital, where she had been born;—and the moments passed pleasantly for Itō, as he listened to her fresh prattle. Presently, at

---

64   August-residence servant.

a turn in the road, they entered a hamlet, densely shadowed by a grove of young trees.

[Here I must interrupt the story to tell you that, without having actually seen them, you cannot imagine how dark some Japanese country villages remain even in the brightest and hottest weather. In the neighborhood of Tōkyō itself there are many villages of this kind. At a short distance from such a settlement you see no houses: nothing is visible but a dense grove of ever-green trees. The grove, which is usually composed of young cedars and bamboos, serves to shelter the village from storms, and also to supply timber for various purposes. So closely are the trees planted that there is no room to pass between the trunks of them: they stand straight as masts, and mingle their crests so as to form a roof that excludes the sun. Each thatched cottage occupies a clear space in the plantation, the trees forming a fence about it, double the height of the building. Under the trees it is always twilight, even at high noon; and the houses, morning or evening, are half in shadow. What makes the first impression of such a village almost disquieting is, not the trans-parent gloom, which has a certain weird charm of its own, but the stillness. There may be fifty or a hundred dwellings; but you see nobody; and you hear no sound but the twitter of invisible birds, the occasional crowing of cocks, and the shrilling of cicadæ. Even the cicadæ, however, find these groves too dim, and sing faintly; being sun-lovers, they prefer the trees outside the village. I forgot to say that you may sometimes hear a viewless shut-tle—*chaka-ton, chaka-ton*;—but that familiar sound, in the great green silence, seems an elfish happening. The reason of the hush is simply that the people are not at home. All the adults, excepting some feeble elders, have gone to the neighboring fields, the women carrying their babies on their backs; and most the chil-dren have gone to the nearest school, perhaps not less than a mile away. Verily, in these dim hushed villages, one seems to behold the mysterious perpetuation of conditions recorded in the texts of Kwang-Tze:—

"*The ancients who had the nourishment of the world wished for nothing, and the world had enough:—they did nothing, and all things were transformed:—their stillness was abysmal, and the people were all composed.*"]

... The village was very dark when Itō reached it; for the sun had set, and the after-glow made no twilight in the shadowing of the trees. "Now, kind sir," the child said, pointing to a narrow lane opening upon the main road, "I have to go this way."

"Permit me, then, to see you home," Itō responded; and he turned into the lane with her, feeling rather than seeing his way. But the girl soon stopped before a small gate, dimly visible in the gloom—a gate of trelliswork, beyond which the lights of a dwelling could be seen. "Here," she said, "is the honorable residence in which I serve. As you have come thus far out of your way, kind sir, will you not deign to enter and to rest a while?" Itō assented. He was pleased by the informal invitation; and he wished to learn what persons of superior condition had chosen to reside in so lonesome a village. He knew that sometimes a family of rank would retire in this manner from public life, by reason of government displeasure or political trouble; and he imagined that such might be the history of the occupants of the dwelling before him. Passing the gate, which his young guide opened for him, he found himself in a large quaint garden. A miniature landscape, traversed by a winding stream, was faintly distinguishable. "Deign for one little moment to wait," the child said; "I go to announce the honorable coming;" and hurried toward the house. It was a spacious house, but seemed very old, and built in the fashion of another time. The sliding doors were not closed; but the lighted interior was concealed by a beautiful bamboo curtain extending along the gallery front. Behind it shadows were moving—shadows of women;—and suddenly the music of a *koto* rippled into the night. So light and sweet was the playing that Itō could scarcely believe the evidence of his senses. A slumbrous feeling of delight stole over him as he listened—a delight strangely mingled with sadness. He wondered

how any woman could have learned to play thus—wondered
whether the player could be a woman—wondered even whether
he was hearing earthly music; for enchantment seemed to have
entered into his blood with the sound of it.

The soft music ceased; and almost at the same moment Itō
found the little *miya-dzukai* beside him. "Sir," she said, "it is
requested that you will honorably enter." She conducted him to
the entrance, where he removed his sandals; and an aged woman,
whom he thought to be the *Rōjo*, or matron of the household,
came to welcome him at the threshold. The old woman then led
him through many apartments to a large and well-lighted room
in the rear of the house, and with many respectful salutations
requested him to take the place of honor accorded to guests of
distinction. He was surprised by the stateliness of the chamber,
and the curious beauty of its decorations. Presently some
maid-servants brought refreshments; and he noticed that the cups
and other vessels set before him were of rare and costly workmanship, and ornamented with a design indicating the high rank
of the possessor. More and more he wondered what noble person
had chosen this lonely retreat, and what happening could have
inspired the wish for such solitude. But the aged attendant
suddenly interrupted his reflections with the question:

"Am I wrong in supposing that you are Itō Sama, of Uji—Itō
Tatéwaki Norisuké?"

Itō bowed in assent. He had not told his name to the little
miya-dzukai, and the manner of the inquiry startled him.

"Please do not think my question rude," continued the attendant. "An old woman like myself may ask questions without
improper curiosity. When you came to the house, I thought that
I knew your face; and I asked your name only to clear away all
doubt, before speaking of other matters. I have some thing of
moment to tell you. You often pass through this village, and our
young Himégimi-Sama[65] happened one morning to see you going

---

65   A scarcely translatable honorific title compounded of the word
himé (princess) and *kimi* (sovereign, master or mistress, lord or lady,
etc.)

by; and ever since that moment she has been thinking about
you, day and night. Indeed, she thought so much that she became
ill; and we have been very uneasy about her. For that reason I
took means to find out your name and residence; and I was on
the point of sending you a letter when—so unexpectedly!—you
came to our gate with the little attendant. Now, to say how happy
I am to see you is not possible; it seems almost too fortunate a
happening to be true! Really I think that this meeting must have
been brought about by the favor of Enmusubi-no-Kami—that
great God of Izumo who ties the knots of fortunate union. And
now that so lucky a destiny has led you hither, perhaps you will
not refuse—if there be no obstacle in the way of such a union—
to make happy the heart of our Himégimi-Sama?"

For the moment Itō did not know how to reply. If the old
woman had spoken the truth, an extraordinary chance was being
offered to him. Only a great passion could impel the daughter
of a noble house to seek, of her own will, the affection of an
obscure and masterless samurai, possessing neither wealth nor
any sort of prospects. On the other hand, it was not in the
honorable nature of the man to further his own interests by
taking advantage of a feminine weakness. Moreover, the circumstances were disquietingly mysterious. Yet how to decline the
proposal, so unexpectedly made, troubled him not a little. After
a short silence, he replied:—

"There would be no obstacle, as I have no wife, and no
betrothed, and no relation with any woman. Until now I have
lived with my parents; and the matter of my marriage was never
discussed by them. You must know that I am a poor samurai,
without any patron among persons of rank; and I did not wish
to marry until I could find some chance to improve my condition.
As to the proposal which you have done me the very great honor
to make, I can only say that I know myself yet unworthy of the
notice of any noble maiden."

The old woman smiled as if pleased by these words, and
responded:—

"Until you have seen our Himégimi-Sama, it were better that you make no decision. Perhaps you will feel no hesitation after you have seen her. Deign now to come with me, that I may present you to her."

She conducted him to another larger guest-room, where preparations for a feast had been made, and having shown him the place of honor, left him for a moment alone. She returned accompanied by the Himégimi-Sama; and, at the first sight of the young mistress, Itō felt again the strange thrill of wonder and delight that had come to him in the garden, as he listened to the music of the *koto*. Never had he dreamed of so beautiful a being. Light seemed to radiate from her presence, and to shine through her garments, as the light of the moon through flossy clouds; her loosely flowing hair swayed about her as she moved, like the boughs of the drooping willow bestirred by the breezes of spring; her lips were like flowers of the peach besprinkled with morning dew. Itō was bewildered by the vision. He asked himself whether he was not looking upon the person of Amano-kawara-no-Ori-Himé herself—the Weaving-Maiden who dwells by the shining River of Heaven.

Smiling, the aged woman turned to the fair one, who remained speechless, with downcast eyes and flushing cheeks, and said to her:—

"See, my child!—at the moment when we could least have hoped for such a thing, the very person whom you wished to meet has come of his own accord. So fortunate a happening could have been brought about only by the will of the high gods. To think of it makes me weep for joy." And she sobbed aloud. "But now," she continued, wiping away her tears with her sleeve, "it only remains for you both—unless either prove unwilling, which I doubt—to pledge yourselves to each other, and to partake of your wedding feast."

Itō answered by no word: the incomparable vision before him had numbed his will and tied his tongue. Maid-servants entered, bearing dishes and wine: the wedding feast was spread before the pair; and the pledges were given. Itō nevertheless remained as in a trance: the marvel of the adventure, and the wonder of the beauty of the bride, still bewildered him. A gladness, beyond aught that he had ever known before, filled his heart—like a great silence. But gradually he recovered his wonted calm; and thereafter he found himself able to converse without embarrassment. Of the wine he partook freely; and he ventured to speak, in a self-deprecating but merry way, about the doubts and fears that had oppressed him. Meanwhile the bride remained still as moonlight, never lifting her eyes, and replying only by a blush or a smile when he addressed her.

Itō said to the aged attendant:—

"Many times, in my solitary walks, I have passed through this village without knowing of the existence of this honorable dwelling. And ever since entering here, I have been wondering why this noble household should have chosen so lonesome a place of sojourn.... Now that your Himégimi-Sama and I have become pledged to each other, it seems to me a strange thing that I do not yet know the name of her august family."

At this utterance, a shadow passed over the kindly face of the old woman; and the bride, who had yet hardly spoken, turned pale, and appeared to become painfully anxious. After some moments of silence, the aged woman responded:—

"To keep our secret from you much longer would be difficult; and I think that, under any circumstances, you should be made aware of the facts, now that you are one of us. Know then, Sir Itō, that your bride is the daughter of Shigéhira-Kyō, the great and unfortunate San-mi Chüjō."

At those words—"Shigéhira-Kyō, San-mi Chüjō"—the young samurai felt a chill, as of ice, strike through all his veins. Shigéhira-Kyō, the great Heiké general and statesman, had been dust for centuries. And Itō suddenly understood that everything around him—the chamber and the lights and the banquet—was a dream of the past; that the forms before him were not people, but shadows of people dead.

But in another instant the icy chill had passed; and the charm returned, and seemed to deepen about him; and he felt no fear. Though his bride had come to him out of Yomi—out of the place of the Yellow Springs of death—his heart had been wholly won. Who weds a ghost must become a ghost;—yet he knew himself ready to die, not once, but many times, rather than betray by word or look one thought that might bring a shadow of pain to the brow of the beautiful illusion before him. Of the affection proffered he had no misgiving: the truth had been told him when any unloving purpose might better have been served by deception. But these thoughts and emotions passed in a flash, leaving him resolved to accept the strange situation as it had presented itself, and to act just as he would have done if chosen, in the years of Jü-ei, by Shigéhira's daughter.

"Ah, the pity of it!" he exclaimed; "I have heard of the cruel fate of the august Lord Shigéhira."

"Ay," responded the aged woman, sobbing as she spoke;—"it was indeed a cruel fate. His horse, you know, was killed by an arrow, and fell upon him; and when he called for help, those who had lived upon his bounty deserted him in his need. Then he was taken prisoner, and sent to Kamakura, where they treated him shamefully, and at last put him to death.[66] His wife and child—this dear maid here—were then in hiding; for everywhere the Heiké were being sought out and killed. When the news of the Lord Shigéhira's death reached us, the pain proved too great

---

66   Shigéhira, after a brave fight in defense of the capital—then held by the Taïra (or Heiké) party—was surprised and routed by Yoshitsuné, leader of the Minamoto forces. A soldier named Iyénaga, who was a skilled archer, shot down Shigéhira's horse; and Shigéhira fell under the struggling animal. He cried to an attendant to bring another horse; but the man fled. Shigéhira was then captured by Iyénaga, and eventually given up to Yoritomo, head of the Minamoto clan, who caused him to be sent in a cage to Kamakura. There, after sundry humiliations, he was treated for a time with consideration—having been able, by a Chinese poem, to touch even the cruel heart of Yoritomo. But in the following year he was executed by request of the Buddhist priests of Nanto, against whom he had formerly waged war by order of Kiyomori.

for the mother to bear, so the child was left with no one to care for her but me—since her kindred had all perished or disappeared. She was only five years old. I had been her milk-nurse, and I did what I could for her. Year after year we wandered from place to place, traveling in pilgrim-garb.... But these tales of grief are ill-timed," exclaimed the nurse, wiping away her tears;— "pardon the foolish heart of an old woman who cannot forget the past. See! the little maid whom I fostered has now become a Himégimi-Sama indeed!—were we living in the good days of the Emperor Takakura, what a destiny might be reserved for her! However, she has obtained the husband whom she desired; that is the greatest happiness.... But the hour is late. The bridal-chamber has been prepared; and I must now leave you to care for each other until morning."

She rose, and sliding back the screens parting the guest-room from the adjoining chamber, ushered them to their sleeping apartment. Then, with many words of joy and congratulation, she withdrew; and Itō was left alone with his bride.

As they reposed together, Itō said:—

"Tell me, my loved one, when was it that you first wished to have me for your husband."

(For everything appeared so real that he had almost ceased to think of the illusion woven around him.)

She answered, in a voice like a dove's voice:—

"My august lord and husband, it was at the temple of Ishiyama, where I went with my foster-mother, that I saw you for the first time. And because of seeing you, the world became changed to me from that hour and moment. But you do not remember, because our meeting was not in this, your present life: it was very, very long ago. Since that time you have passed through many deaths and births, and have had many comely bodies. But I have remained always that which you see me now: I could not obtain another body, nor enter into another state of existence, because of my great wish for you. My dear lord and husband, I have waited for you through many ages of men."

And the bridegroom felt nowise afraid at hearing these strange words, but desired nothing more in life, or in all his lives to come, than to feel her arms about him, and to hear the caress of her voice.

But the pealing of a temple-bell proclaimed the coming of dawn. Birds began to twitter; a morning breeze set all the trees a-whispering. Suddenly the old nurse pushed apart the sliding screens of the bridal-chamber, and exclaimed:—

"My children, it is time to separate! By daylight you must not be together, even for an instant: that were fatal! You must bid each other good-bye."

Without a word, Itō made ready to depart. He vaguely understood the warning uttered, and resigned himself wholly to destiny. His will belonged to him no more; he desired only to please his shadowy bride.

She placed in his hands a little *suzuri*, or ink-stone, curiously carved, and said:—

"My young lord and husband is a scholar; therefore this small gift will probably not be despised by him. It is of strange fashion because it is old, having been augustly bestowed upon my father by the favor of the Emperor Takakura. For that reason only, I thought it to be a precious thing."

Itō, in return, besought her to accept for a remembrance the *kōgai*[67] of his sword, which were decorated with inlaid work of silver and gold, representing plum-flowers and nightingales.

Then the little *miya-dzukai* came to guide him through the garden, and his bride with her foster-mother accompanied him to the threshold.

As he turned at the foot of the steps to make his parting salute, the old woman said:—

---

67   This was the name given to a pair of metal rods attached to a sword-sheath, and used like chop-sticks. They were sometimes exquisitely ornamented.

"We shall meet again the next Year of the Boar, at the same hour of the same day of the same month that you came here. This being the Year of the Tiger, you will have to wait ten years. But, for reasons which I must not say, we shall not be able to meet again in this place; we are going to the neighborhood of Kyōto, where the good Emperor Takakura and our fathers and many of our people are dwelling. All the Heiké will be rejoiced by your coming. We shall send a *kago*[68] for you on the appointed day."

Above the village the stars were burning as Itō passed the gate; but on reaching the open road he saw the dawn brightening beyond leagues of silent fields. In his bosom he carried the gift of his bride. The charm of her voice lingered in his ears—and nevertheless, had it not been for the memento which he touched with questioning fingers, he could have persuaded himself that the memories of the night were memories of sleep, and that his life still belonged to him.

But the certainty that he had doomed himself evoked no least regret: he was troubled only by the pain of separation, and the thought of the seasons that would have to pass before the illusion could be renewed for him. Ten years!—and every day of those years would seem how long! The mystery of the delay he could not hope to solve; the secret ways of the dead are known to the gods alone.

Often and often, in his solitary walks, Itō revisited the village at Kotobikiyama, vaguely hoping to obtain another glimpse of the past. But never again, by night or by day, was he able to find the rustic gate in the shadowed lane; never again could he perceive the figure of the little miya-dzukai, walking alone in the sunset-glow.

The village people, whom he questioned carefully, thought him bewitched. No person of rank, they said, had ever dwelt in the settlement; and there had never been, in the neighborhood, any such garden as he described. But there had once been a great Buddhist temple near the place of which he spoke; and

---

68   A kind of palanquin.

some gravestones of the temple-cemetery were still to be seen. Itō discovered the monuments in the middle of a dense thicket. They were of an ancient Chinese form, and were covered with moss and lichens. The characters that had been cut upon them could no longer be deciphered.

Of his adventure Itō spoke to no one. But friends and kindred soon perceived a great change in his appearance and manner. Day by day he seemed to become more pale and thin, though physicians declared that he had no bodily ailment; he looked like a ghost, and moved like a shadow. Thoughtful and solitary he had always been, but now he appeared indifferent to everything which had formerly given him pleasure—even to those literary studies by means of which he might have hoped to win distinction. To his mother—who thought that marriage might quicken his former ambition, and revive his interest in life—he said that he had made a vow to marry no living woman. And the months dragged by.

At last came the Year of the Boar, and the season of autumn; but Itō could no longer take the solitary walks that he loved. He could not even rise from his bed. His life was ebbing, though none could divine the cause; and he slept so deeply and so long that his sleep was often mistaken for death.

Out of such a sleep he was startled, one bright evening, by the voice of a child; and he saw at his bedside the little *miya-dzukai* who had guided him, ten years before, to the gate of the vanished garden. She saluted him, and smiled, and said: "I am bidden to tell you that you will be received to-night at Ōhara, near Kyōto, where the new home is, and that a *kago* has been sent for you." Then she disappeared.

Itō knew that he was being summoned away from the light of the sun; but the message so rejoiced him that he found strength to sit up and call his mother. To her he then for the first time related the story of his bridal, and he showed her the ink-stone which had been given him. He asked that it should be placed in his coffin—and then he died.

The ink-stone was buried with him. But before the funeral ceremonies it was examined by experts, who said that it had been made in the period of Jō-an (AD1169), and that it bore the seal-mark of an artist who had lived in the time of the Emperor Takakura

OSHIDORI

There was a falconer and hunter, named Sonjō, who lived in the district called Tamura-no-Gō, of the province of Mutsu. One day he went out hunting, and could not find any game. But on his way home, at a place called Akanuma, he perceived a pair of *oshidori*[69] (mandarin-ducks), swimming together in a river that he was about to cross. To kill *oshidori* is not good; but Sonjō happened to be very hungry, and he shot at the pair. His arrow pierced the male: the female escaped into the rushes of the further shore, and disappeared. Sonjō took the dead bird home, and cooked it.

That night he dreamed a dreary dream. It seemed to him that a beautiful woman came into his room, and stood by his pillow, and began to weep. So bitterly did she weep that Sonjō felt as if his heart were being torn out while he listened. And the woman cried to him: "Why—oh! Why did you kill him?—of what wrong was he guilty?... At Akanuma we were so happy together—and you killed him!... What harm did he ever do you? Do you even know what you have done?—oh! Do you know what a cruel, what a wicked thing you have done?... Me too you have killed—for I will not live without my husband!... Only to tell you this I came."... Then again she wept aloud—so bitterly that the voice of her crying pierced into the marrow of the listener's bones;—and she sobbed out the words of this poem:—

Hi kururéba
Sasoëshi mono wo—
Akanuma no
Makomo no kuré no
Hitori-né zo uki![70]

---

69   From ancient times, in the Far East, these birds have been regarded as emblems of conjugal affection.

70   There is a pathetic double meaning in the third verse; for the syllables composing the proper name Akanuma ("Red Marsh") may also be read as *akanu-ma*, signifying "the time of our inseparable (or

And after having uttered these verses she exclaimed:—"Ah, you do not know—you cannot know what you have done! But to-morrow, when you go to Akanuma, you will see—you will see…" So saying, and weeping very piteously, she went away.

When Sonjō awoke in the morning, this dream remained so vivid in his mind that he was greatly troubled. He remembered the words:—"But to-morrow, when you go to Akanuma, you will see—you will see." And he resolved to go there at once, that he might learn whether his dream was anything more than a dream.

So he went to Akanuma; and there, when he came to the river-bank, he saw the female *oshidori* swimming alone. In the same moment the bird perceived Sonjō; but, instead of trying to escape, she swam straight towards him, looking at him the while in a strange fixed way. Then, with her beak, she suddenly tore open her own body, and died before the hunter's eyes…

Sonjō shaved his head, and became a priest.

---

delightful) relation." So the poem can also be thus rendered:—"When the day began to fail, I had invited him to accompany me…! Now, after the time of that happy relation, what misery for the one who must slumber alone in the shadow of the rushes!"—The *makomo* is a short of large rush, used for making baskets.

THE SYMPATHY OF BENTEN

In Kyōto there is a famous temple called Amadera. Sadazumi Shinnō, the fifth son of the Emperor Seiwa, passed the greater part of his life there as a priest; and the graves of many celebrated persons are to be seen in the temple-grounds.

But the present edifice is not the ancient Amadera. The original temple, after the lapse of ten centuries, fell into such decay that it had to be entirely rebuilt in the fourteenth year of Genroku (AD 1701).

A great festival was held to celebrate the rebuilding of the Amadera; and among the thousands of persons who attended that festival there was a young scholar and poet named Hanagaki Baishū. He wandered about the newly laid-out grounds and gardens, delighted by all that he saw, until he reached the place of a spring at which he had often drunk in former times. He was then surprised to find that the soil about the spring had been dug away, so as to form a square pond, and that at one corner of this pond there had been set up a wooden tablet bearing the words *Tanj -Sui* ("Birth-Water").[71] He also saw that a small, but very handsome temple of the Goddess Benten had been erected beside the pond. While he was looking at this new temple, a sudden gust of wind blew to his feet a *tanzaku*,[72] on which the following poem had been written:—

Shirushi aréto
Iwai zo somuru

---

71   The word *tanjō* (birth) should here be understood in its mystical Buddhist meaning of new life or rebirth, rather than in the Western signification of birth.

72   *Tanzaku* is the name given to the long strips or ribbons of paper, usually colored, upon which poems are written perpendicularly. Poems written upon *tanzaku* are suspended to trees in flower, to wind-bells, to any beautiful object in which the poet has found an inspiration.

Tama hōki,
Toruté bakari no
Chigiri narétomo.

This poem—a poem on first love (*hatsu koi*), composed by the famous Shunrei Kyō—was not unfamiliar to him; but it had been written upon the *tanzaku* by a female hand, and so exquisitely that he could scarcely believe his eyes. Something in the form of the characters—an indefinite grace—suggested that period of youth between childhood and womanhood; and the pure rich color of the ink seemed to bespeak the purity and goodness of the writer's heart.[73]

Baishū carefully folded up the *tanzaku*, and took it home with him. When he looked at it again the writing appeared to him even more wonderful than at first. His knowledge in calligraphy assured him only that the poem had been written by some girl who was very young, very intelligent, and probably very gentle-hearted. But this assurance sufficed to shape within his mind the image of a very charming person; and he soon found himself in love with the unknown. Then his first resolve was to seek out the writer of the verses, and, if possible, make her his wife.... Yet how was he to find her? Who was she? Where did she live? Certainly he could hope to find her only through the favor of the Gods.

But presently it occurred to him that the Gods might be very willing to lend their aid. The *tanzaku* had come to him while he was standing in front of the temple of Benten-Sama; and it was to this divinity in particular that lovers were wont to pray

---

73   It is difficult for the inexperienced European eye to distinguish in Chinese or Japanese writing those characteristics implied by our term "hand"—in the sense of individual style. But the Japanese scholar never forgets the peculiarities of a handwriting once seen; and he can even guess at the approximate age of the writer. Chinese and Japanese authors claim that the color (quality) of the ink used tells something of the character of the writer. As every person grounds or prepares his or her own ink, the deeper and clearer black would at least indicate something of personal carefulness and of the sense of beauty.

for happy union. This reflection impelled him to beseech the Goddess for assistance. He went at once to the temple of Benten-of-the-Birth-Water (*Tanj -sui-no-Benten*) in the grounds of the Amadera; and there, with all the fervor of his heart, he made his petition:—"O Goddess, pity me!—help me to find where the young person lives who wrote the *tanzaku*!—vouchsafe me but one chance to meet her—even if only for a moment!" And after having made this prayer, he began to perform a seven days' religious service (*nanuka-mairi*)[74] in honor of the Goddess; vowing at the same time to pass the seventh night in ceaseless worship before her shrine.

Now on the seventh night—the night of his vigil—during the hour when the silence is most deep, he heard at the main gateway of the temple-grounds a voice calling for admittance. Another voice from within answered; the gate was opened; and Baishū saw an old man of majestic appearance approaching with slow steps. This venerable person was clad in robes of ceremony; and he wore upon his snow-white head a black cap (*eboshi*) of the form indicating high rank. Reaching the little temple of Benten, he knelt down in front of it, as if respectfully awaiting some order. Then the outer door of the temple was opened; the hanging curtain of bamboo behind it, concealing the inner sanctuary, was rolled half-way up; and a *chigo*[75] came forward—a beautiful boy, with long hair tied back in the ancient manner. He stood at the threshold, and said to the old man in a clear loud voice:—

"There is a person here who has been praying for a love-union not suitable to his present condition, and otherwise difficult to bring about. But as the young man is worthy of Our pity, you have been called to see whether something can be done for him.

---

74   There are many kinds of religious exercises called *mairi*. The performer of a *nanuka-mairi* pledges himself to pray at a certain temple every day for seven days in succession.

75   The term *chigo* usually means the page of a noble household, especially an Imperial page. The *chigo* who appears in this story is of course a supernatural being—the court-messenger of the Goddess, and her mouthpiece.

If there should prove to be any relation between the parties from the period of a former birth, you will introduce them to each other."

On receiving this command, the old man bowed respectfully to the *chigo*: then, rising, he drew from the pocket of his long left sleeve a crimson cord. One end of this cord he passed round Baishū's body, as if to bind him with it. The other end he put into the flame of one of the temple-lamps; and while the cord was there burning, he waved his hand three times, as if to summon somebody out of the dark.

Immediately, in the direction of the Amadera, a sound of coming steps was heard; and in another moment a girl appeared—a charming girl, fifteen or sixteen years old. She approached gracefully, but very shyly—hiding the lower part of her face with a fan; and she knelt down beside Baishū. The *chigo* then said to Baishū:—

"Recently you have been suffering much heart-pain; and this desperate love of yours has even impaired your health. We could not allow you to remain in so unhappy a condition; and We therefore summoned the Old-Man-under-the-Moon[76] to make you acquainted with the writer of that *tanzaku*. She is now beside you."

With these words, the *chigo* retired behind the bamboo curtain. Then the old man went away as he had come; and the young girl followed him. Simultaneously Baishū heard the great bell of the Amadera sounding the hour of dawn. He prostrated himself in thanksgiving before the shrine of Benten-of-the-Birth-Water, and proceeded homeward—feeling as if awakened from some delightful dream—happy at having seen the charming person whom he had so fervently prayed to meet—unhappy also because of the fear that he might never meet her again.

But scarcely had he passed from the gateway into the street, when he saw a young girl walking alone in the same direction

---

76   *Gekkawō*. This is a poetical appellation for the God of Marriage, more usually known as *Musubi-no-kami*. Throughout this story there is an interesting mingling of Shintō and Buddhist ideas.

that he was going; and, even in the dusk of the dawn, he recognized her at once as the person to whom he had been introduced before the temple of Benten. As he quickened his pace to overtake her, she turned and saluted him with a graceful bow. Then for the first time he ventured to speak to her; and she answered him in a voice of which the sweetness filled his heart with joy. Through the yet silent streets they walked on, chatting happily, till they found themselves before the house where Baishū lived. There he paused—spoke to the girl of his hopes and fears. Smiling, she asked:—"Do you not know that I was sent for to become your wife?" And she entered with him.

Becoming his wife, she delighted him beyond expectation by the charm of her mind and heart. Moreover, he found her to be much more accomplished than he had supposed. Besides being able to write so wonderfully, she could paint beautiful pictures; she knew the art of arranging flowers, the art of embroidery, the art of music; she could weave and sew; and she knew everything in regard to the management of a house.

It was in the early autumn that the young people had met; and they lived together in perfect accord until the winter season began. Nothing, during those months, occurred to disturb their peace. Baishū's love for his gentle wife only strengthened with the passing of time. Yet, strangely enough, he remained ignorant of her history—knew nothing about her family. Of such matters she had never spoken; and, as the Gods had given her to him, he imagined that it would not be proper to question her. But neither the Old-Man-under-the-Moon nor any one else came—as he had feared—to take her away. Nobody even made any inquiries about her. And the neighbors, for some undiscoverable reason, acted as if totally unaware of her presence.

Baishū wondered at all this. But stranger experiences were awaiting him.

One winter morning he happened to be passing through a somewhat remote quarter of the city, when he heard himself loudly called by name, and saw a man-servant making signs to him from the gateway of a private residence. As Baishū did not know the man's face, and did not have a single acquaintance in that part of Kyōto, he was more than startled by so abrupt a summons. But the servant, coming forward, saluted him with the utmost respect, and said, "My master greatly desires the honor of speaking with you: deign to enter for a moment." After an instant of hesitation, Baish allowed himself to be conducted to the house. A dignified and richly dressed person, who seemed to be the master, welcomed him at the entrance, and led him to the guest-room. When the courtesies due upon a first meeting had been fully exchanged, the host apologized for the informal manner of his invitation, and said:—

"It must have seemed to you very rude of us to call you in such a way. But perhaps you will pardon our impoliteness when I tell you that we acted thus upon what I firmly believe to have been an inspiration from the Goddess Benten. Now permit me to explain.

"I have a daughter, about sixteen years old, who can write rather well,[77] and do other things in the common way: she has the ordinary nature of woman. As we were anxious to make her happy by finding a good husband for her, we prayed the Goddess Benten to help us; and we sent to every temple of Benten in the city a *tanzaku* written by the girl. Some nights later, the Goddess appeared to me in a dream, and said: 'We have heard your prayer, and have already introduced your daughter to the person who is to become her husband. During the coming winter he will visit you.' As I did not understand this assurance that a presentation had been made, I felt some doubt; I thought that the dream might have been only a common dream, signifying nothing. But last night again I saw Benten-Sama in a dream; and

77   As it is the old Japanese rule that parents should speak depreciatingly of their children's accomplishments the phrase "rather well" in this connection would mean, for the visitor, "wonderfully well." For the same reason the expressions "common way" and "ordinary nature," as subsequently used, would imply almost the reverse of the literal meaning.

she said to me: 'To-morrow the young man, of whom I once spoke to you, will come to this street: then you can call him into your house, and ask him to become the husband of your daughter. He is a good young man; and later in life he will obtain a much higher rank than he now holds.' Then Benten-Sama told me your name, your age, your birthplace, and described your features and dress so exactly that my servant found no difficulty in recognizing you by the indications which I was able to give him."

This explanation bewildered Baishū instead of reassuring him; and his only reply was a formal return of thanks for the honor which the master of the house had spoken of doing him. But when the host invited him to another room, for the purpose of presenting him to the young lady, his embarrassment became extreme. Yet he could not reasonably decline the introduction. He could not bring himself, under such extraordinary circumstances, to announce that he already had a wife—a wife given to him by the Goddess Benten herself; a wife from whom he could not even think of separating. So, in silence and trepidation, he followed his host to the apartment indicated.

Then what was his amazement to discover, when presented to the daughter of the house, that she was the very same person whom he had already taken to wife!

The same—yet not the same.

She to whom he had been introduced by the Old-Man-under-the-Moon, was only the soul of the beloved.

She to whom he was now to be wedded, in her father's house, was the body.

Benten had wrought this miracle for the sake of her worshippers.

The original story breaks off suddenly at this point, leaving several matters unexplained. The ending is rather unsatisfactory. One would like to know something about the mental experiences of the real maiden during the married life of her phantom. One would also like to know what became of the phantom—whether it continued to lead an independent existence; whether it waited patiently for the return of its husband; whether it paid a visit to the real bride. And the book says nothing about these things. But a Japanese friend explains the miracle thus:—

"The spirit-bride was really formed out of the *tanzaku*. So it is possible that the real girl did not know anything about the meeting at the temple of Benten. When she wrote those beautiful characters upon the *tanzaku*, something of her spirit passed into them. Therefore it was possible to evoke from the writing the double of the writer."

THE GOBLIN-SPIDER

In very ancient books it is said that there used to be many goblin-spiders in Japan.

Some folks declare there are still some goblin-spiders. During the daytime they look just like common spiders; but very late at night, when everybody is asleep, and there is no sound, they become very, very big, and do awful things. Goblin-spiders are supposed also to have the magical power of taking human shape—so as to deceive people. And there is a famous Japanese story about such a spider.

There was once, in some lonely part of the country, a haunted temple. No one could live in the building because of the goblins that had taken possession of it. Many brave samurai went to that place at various times for the purpose of killing the goblins. But they were never heard of again after they had entered the temple.

At last one who was famous for his courage and his prudence, went to the temple to watch during the night. And he said to those who accompanied him there:—"If in the morning I am still alive, I shall drum upon the drum of the temple." Then he was left alone, to watch by the light of a lamp.

As the night advanced he crouched down under the altar, which supported a dusty image of Buddha. He saw nothing strange and heard no sound till after midnight. Then there came a goblin, having but half a body and one eye, and said:"*Hitokusai!*" ["There is the smell of a man!"] But the samurai did not move. The goblin went away.

Then there came a priest and played upon a *samisen* so wonderfully that the samurai felt sure it was not the playing of a man. So he leaped up with his sword drawn. The priest, seeing him, burst out laughing, and said:—"So you thought I was a goblin? Oh no! I am only the priest of this temple; but I have to play to keep off the goblins. Does not this *samisen* sound well? Please play a little."

And he offered the instrument to the samurai who grasped it very cautiously with his left hand. But instantly the *samisen* changed into a monstrous spider web, and the priest into a goblin and the warrior found himself caught fast in the web by the left hand. He struggled bravely, and struck at the spider with his sword, and wounded it; but he soon became entangled still more in the net, and could not move.

However, the wounded spider crawled away—and the sun rose. In a little while the people came and found the samurai in the horrible web, and freed him. They saw tracks of blood upon the floor, and followed the tracks out of the temple to a hole in the deserted garden. Out of the hole issued a frightful sound of groaning. They found the wounded goblin in the hole, and killed it.

MUJINA

On the Akasaka Road, in Tōkyō, there is a slope called Kii-no-kuni-zaka—which means the Slope of the Province of Kii. I do not know why it is called the Slope of the Province of Kii. On one side of this slope you see an ancient moat, deep and very wide, with high green banks rising up to some place of gardens;—and on the other side of the road extend the long and lofty walls of an imperial palace. Before the era of street-lamps and *jinrikishas*, this neighborhood was very lonesome after dark; and belated pedestrians would go miles out of their way rather than mount the Kii-no-kuni-zaka, alone, after sunset.

All because of a Mujina that used to walk there.[78]

The last man who saw the Mujina was an old merchant of the Kyōbashi quarter, who died about thirty years ago. This is the story, as he told it:—

One night, at a late hour, he was hurrying up the Kii-no-kuni-zaka, when he perceived a woman crouching by the moat, all alone, and weeping bitterly. Fearing that she intended to drown herself, he stopped to offer her any assistance or consolation in his power. She appeared to be a slight and graceful person, handsomely dressed; and her hair was arranged like that of a young girl of good family. "O-jochū,"[79] he exclaimed, approaching her—"O-jochū, do not cry like that!... Tell me what the trouble is; and if there be any way to help you, I shall be glad to help you." (He really meant what he said; for he was a very kind man.) But she continued to weep—hiding her face from him with one of her long sleeves. "O-jochū," he said again, as gently as he could—"please, please listen to me!...This is no place for a young lady at night! Do not cry, I implore you!—only tell me how I

---

78   A kind of badger. Certain animals were thought to be able to transform themselves and cause mischief for humans.

79   O-jochū ("honorable damsel"), a polite form of address used in speaking to a young lady whom one does not know.

may be of some help to you!" Slowly she rose up, but turned her back to him, and continued to moan and sob behind her sleeve. He laid his hand lightly upon her shoulder, and pleaded:— "O-jochū!—O-jochū!—O-jochū!... Listen to me, just for one little moment!... O-jochū!—O-jochū!"... Then that O-jochū turned around, and dropped her sleeve, and stroked her face with her hand;—and the man saw that she had no eyes or nose or mouth— and he screamed and ran away.[80]

Up Kii-no-kuni-zaka he ran and ran; and all was black and empty before him. On and on he ran, never daring to look back; and at last he saw a lantern, so far away that it looked like the gleam of a firefly; and he made for it. It proved to be only the lantern of an itinerant *soba*-seller,[81] who had set down his stand by the road-side; but any light and any human companionship was good after that experience; and he flung himself down at the feet of the soba-seller, crying out, "Ah!—aa!!—*aa!!!*"...

"*Kore! Kore!*"[82] roughly exclaimed the *soba*-man. "Here! What is the matter with you? Anybody hurt you?"

"No—nobody hurt me," panted the other—"only... *Ah!—aa!*"

"—Only scared you?" queried the peddler, unsympathetically. "Robbers?"

"Not robbers—not robbers," gasped the terrified man... "I saw... I saw a woman—by the moat;—and she showed me... *Ah!* I cannot tell you what she showed me!"...

"*He!*[83] Was it anything like this that she showed you?" cried the *soba*-man, stroking his own face—which therewith became like unto an Egg... And, simultaneously, the light went out.

---

80   An apparition with a smooth, totally featureless face, called a "*nopperabo*," is a stock part of the Japanese pantheon of ghosts and demons.

81   *Soba* is a preparation of buckwheat, somewhat resembling vermicelli.

82   An exclamation of annoyed alarm.

83   Well!

THE GRATITUDE OF THE
SAMÉBITO

There was a man named Tawaraya Tōtarō, who lived in the Province of Ōmi. His house was situated on the shore of Lake Biwa, not far from the famous temple called Ishiyamadera. He had some property, and lived in comfort; but at the age of twenty-nine he was still unmarried. His greatest ambition was to marry a very beautiful woman; and he had not been able to find a girl to his liking.

One day, as he was passing over the Long Bridge of Séta,[84] he saw a strange being crouching close to the parapet. The body of this being resembled the body of a man, but was black as ink; its face was like the face of a demon; its eyes were green as emeralds; and its beard was like the beard of a dragon. Tōtarō was at first very much startled. But the green eyes looked at him so gently that after a moment's hesitation he ventured to question the creature. Then it answered him, saying: "I am a *Samébito*,[85]—a Shark-Man of the sea; and until a short time ago I was in the service of the Eight Great Dragon-Kings [*Hachi-Dai-Ryū-Ō*] as a subordinate officer in the Dragon-Palace [*Ryūgū*].[86] But because

---

84   The Long Bridge of Séta (*Séta-no-Naga-Hashi*), famous in Japanese legend, is nearly eight hundred feet in length, and commands a beautiful view. This bridge crosses the waters of the Sétagawa near the junction of the stream with Lake Biwa. Ishiyamadera, one of the most picturesque Buddhist temples in Japan, is situated within a short distance from the bridge.

85   Literally, "a Shark-Person," but in this story the *Samébito* is a male. The characters for *Samébito* can also be read *Kōjin*—which is the usual reading. In dictionaries the word is loosely rendered by "merman" or "mermaid;" but as the above description shows, the *Samébito* or *Kōjin* of the Far East is a conception having little in common with the Western idea of a merman or mermaid.

86   *Ryūgū* is also the name given to the whole of that fairy-realm beneath the sea which figures in so many Japanese legends.

of a small fault which I committed, I was dismissed from the Dragon-Palace, and also banished from the Sea. Since then I have been wandering about here—unable to get any food, or even a place to lie down. If you can feel any pity for me, do, I beseech you, help me to find a shelter, and let me have something to eat!"

This petition was uttered in so plaintive a tone, and in so humble a manner, that Tōtarō's heart was touched. "Come with me," he said. "There is in my garden a large and deep pond where you may live as long as you wish; and I will give you plenty to eat."

The *Samébito* followed Tōtarō home, and appeared to be much pleased with the pond.

Thereafter, for nearly half a year, this strange guest dwelt in the pond, and was every day supplied by Tōtarō with such food as sea-creatures like.

[*From this point of the original narrative the Shark-Man is referred to, not as a monster, but as a sympathetic Person of the male sex.*]

Now, in the seventh month of the same year, there was a female pilgrimage (nyonin-m dé) to the great Buddhist temple called Miidera, in the neighboring town of Ōtsu; and Tōtarō went to Ōtsu to attend the festival. Among the multitude of women and young girls there assembled, he observed a person of extraordinary beauty. She seemed about sixteen years old; her face was fair and pure as snow; and the loveliness of her lips assured the beholder that their every utterance would sound "as sweet as the voice of a nightingale singing upon a plum-tree." Tōtarō fell in love with her at sight. When she left the temple he followed her at a respectful distance, and discovered that she and her mother were staying for a few days at a certain house in the neighboring village of Séta. By questioning some of the village folk, he was able also to learn that her name was Tamana; that she was unmarried; and that her family appeared to be unwilling that she should marry a man of ordinary rank—for they demanded as a betrothal-gift a casket containing ten thousand jewels.[87]

Tōtarō returned home very much dismayed by this information. The more that he thought about the strange betrothal-gift demanded by the girl's parents, the more he felt that he could never expect to obtain her for his wife. Even supposing that there were as many as ten thousand jewels in the whole country, only a great prince could hope to procure them.

But not even for a single hour could Tōtarō banish from his mind the memory of that beautiful being. It haunted him so that he could neither eat nor sleep; and it seemed to become more and more vivid as the days went by. And at last he became ill— so ill that he could not lift his head from the pillow. Then he sent for a doctor.

The doctor, after having made a careful examination, uttered an exclamation of surprise. "Almost any kind of sickness," he said, "can be cured by proper medical treatment, except the sickness of love. Your ailment is evidently love-sickness. There is no cure for it. In ancient times Rōya-Ō Hakuyo died of that sickness; and you must prepare yourself to die as he died." So saying, the doctor went away, without even giving any medicine to Tōtarō.

About this time the Shark-Man that was living in the garden-pond heard of his master's sickness, and came into the house to wait upon Tōtarō. And he tended him with the utmost affection both by day and by night. But he did not know either the cause or the serious nature of the sickness until nearly a week later, when Tōtarō, thinking himself about to die, uttered these words of farewell:—

"I suppose that I have had the pleasure of caring for you thus long, because of some relation that grew up between us in a

87   *Tama* in the original. This word *tama* has a multitude of meanings; and as here used it is quite as indefinite as our own terms "jewel," "gem," or "precious stone." Indeed, it is more indefinite, for it signifies also a bead of coral, a ball of crystal, a polished stone attached to a hairpin, etc. Later on, however, I venture to render it by "ruby,"—for reasons which need no explanation.

former state of existence. But now I am very sick indeed, and every day my sickness becomes worse; and my life is like the morning dew which passes away before the setting of the sun. For your sake, therefore, I am troubled in mind. Your existence has depended upon my care; and I fear that there will be no one to care for you and to feed you when I am dead.... My poor friend!...Alas! our hopes and our wishes are always disappointed in this unhappy world!"

No sooner had Tōtarō spoken these words than the *Samébito* uttered a strange wild cry of pain, and began to weep bitterly. And as he wept, great tears of blood streamed from his green eyes and rolled down his black cheeks and dripped upon the floor. And, falling, they were blood; but, having fallen, they became hard and bright and beautiful—became jewels of inestimable price, rubies splendid as crimson fire. For when men of the sea weep, their tears become precious stones.

Then Tōtarō, beholding this marvel, was so amazed and over-joyed that his strength returned to him. He sprang from his bed, and began to pick up and to count the tears of the Shark-Man, crying out the while: "My sickness is cured! I shall live! I shall live!"

Therewith, the Shark-Man, greatly astonished, ceased to weep, and asked Tōtarō to explain this wonderful cure; and Tōtarō told him about the young person seen at Miidera, and about the extraordinary marriage-gift demanded by her family. "As I felt sure," added Tōtarō, "that I should never be able to get ten thousand jewels, I supposed that my suit would be hopeless. Then I became very unhappy, and at last fell sick. But now, because of your generous weeping, I have many precious stones; and I think that I shall be able to marry that girl. Only—there are not yet quite enough stones; and I beg that you will be good enough to weep a little more, so as to make up the full number required."

But at this request the *Samébito* shook his head, and answered in a tone of surprise and of reproach:—

"Do you think that I am like a harlot—able to weep whenever I wish? Oh, no! Harlots shed tears in order to deceive men; but creatures of the sea cannot weep without feeling real sorrow. I wept for you because of the true grief that I felt in my heart at the thought that you were going to die. But now I cannot weep for you, because you have told me that your sickness is cured."

"Then what am I to do?" plaintively asked Tōtarō. "Unless I can get ten thousand jewels, I cannot marry the girl!"

The *Samébito* remained for a little while silent, as if thinking. Then he said:—

"Listen! To-day I cannot possibly weep any more. But to-morrow let us go together to the Long Bridge of Séta, taking with us some wine and some fish. We can rest for a time on the bridge; and while we are drinking the wine and eating the fish, I shall gaze in the direction of the Dragon-Palace, and try, by thinking of the happy days that I spent there, to make myself feel homesick—so that I can weep."

Tōtarō joyfully assented.

Next morning the two, taking plenty of wine and fish with them, went to the Séta bridge, and rested there, and feasted. After having drunk a great deal of wine, the *Samébito* began to gaze in the direction of the Dragon-Kingdom, and to think about the past. And gradually, under the softening influence of the wine, the memory of happier days filled his heart with sorrow, and the pain of homesickness came upon him, so that he could weep profusely. And the great red tears that he shed fell upon the bridge in a shower of rubies; and Tōtarō gathered them as they fell, and put them into a casket, and counted them until he had counted the full number of ten thousand. Then he uttered a shout of joy.

Almost in the same moment, from far away over the lake, a delightful sound of music was heard; and there appeared in the offing, slowly rising from the waters, like some fabric of cloud, a palace of the color of the setting sun.

At once the Samébito sprang upon the parapet of the bridge, and looked, and laughed for joy. Then, turning to Tōtarō, he said:—

"There must have been a general amnesty proclaimed in the Dragon-Realm; the Kings are calling me. So now I must bid you farewell. I am happy to have had one chance of befriending you in return for your goodness to me."

With these words he leaped from the bridge; and no man ever saw him again. But Tōtarō presented the casket of red jewels to the parents of Tamana, and so obtained her in marriage.

FRAGMENT

And it was at the hour of sunset that they came to the foot of the mountain. There was in that place no sign of life—neither token of water, nor trace of plant, nor shadow of flying bird—nothing but desolation rising to desolation. And the summit was lost in heaven.

Then the Bodhisattva said to his young companion:—"What you have asked to see will be shown to you. But the place of the Vision is far; and the way is rude. Follow after me, and do not fear: strength will be given you."

Twilight gloomed about them as they climbed. There was no beaten path, nor any mark of former human visitation; and the way was over an endless heaping of tumbled fragments that rolled or turned beneath the foot. Sometimes a mass dislodged would clatter down with hollow echoings;—sometimes the substance trodden would burst like an empty shell.... Stars pointed and thrilled; and the darkness deepened.

"Do not fear, my son," said the Bodhisattva, guiding: "danger there is none, though the way be grim."

Under the stars they climbed—fast, fast—mounting by help of power superhuman. High zones of mist they passed; and they saw below them, ever widening as they climbed, a soundless flood of cloud, like the tide of a milky sea.

Hour after hour they climbed;—and forms invisible yielded to their tread with dull soft crashings;—and faint cold fires lighted and died at every breaking.

And once the pilgrim-youth laid hand on a something smooth that was not stone—and lifted it—and dimly saw the cheekless gibe of death.

"Linger not thus, my son!" urged the voice of the teacher;—"the summit that we must gain is very far away!"

On through the dark they climbed—and felt continually beneath them the soft strange breakings—and saw the icy fires worm and die—till the rim of the night turned grey, and the stars began to fail, and the east began to bloom.

Yet still they climbed—fast, fast—mounting by help of power superhuman. About them now was frigidness of death—and silence tremendous....A gold flame kindled in the east.

Then first to the pilgrim's gaze the steeps revealed their nakedness;—and a trembling seized him—and a ghastly fear. For there was not any ground—neither beneath him nor about him nor above him—but a heaping only, monstrous and measureless, of skulls and fragments of skulls and dust of bone—with a shimmer of shed teeth strown through the drift of it, like the shimmer of scrags of shell in the wrack of a tide.

"Do not fear, my son!" cried the voice of the Bodhisattva;—"only the strong of heart can win to the place of the Vision!"

Behind them the world had vanished. Nothing remained but the clouds beneath, and the sky above, and the heaping of skulls between—up-slanting out of sight.

Then the sun climbed with the climbers; and there was no warmth in the light of him, but coldness sharp as a sword. And the horror of stupendous height, and the nightmare of stupendous depth, and the terror of silence, ever grew and grew, and weighed upon the pilgrim, and held his feet—so that suddenly all power departed from him, and he moaned like a sleeper in dreams.

"Hasten, hasten, my son!" cried the Bodhisattva: "the day is brief, and the summit is very far away."

But the pilgrim shrieked—"I fear! I fear unspeakably!—and the power has departed from me!"

"The power will return, my son," made answer the Bodhisattva.... "Look now below you and above you and about you, and tell me what you see."

"I cannot," cried the pilgrim, trembling and clinging; "I dare not look beneath! Before me and about me there is nothing but skulls of men."

"And yet, my son," said the Bodhisattva, laughing softly—"and yet you do not know of what this mountain is made."

The other, shuddering, repeated:—"I fear!—unutterably I fear!... there is nothing but skulls of men!"

"A mountain of skulls it is," responded the Bodhisattva. "But know, my son, that all of them are your own! Each has at some time been the nest of your dreams and delusions and desires. Not even one of them is the skull of any other being. All—all without exception—have been yours, in the billions of your former lives."

NOCTILUCAE

The moon had not yet risen; but the vast of the night was all seething with stars, and bridged by a Milky Way of extraordinary brightness. There was no wind; but the sea, far as sight could reach, was running in ripples of fire—a vision of infernal beauty. Only the ripplings were radiant (between them was blackness absolute);—and the luminosity was amazing. Most of the undulations were yellow like candle-flame; but there were crimson lampings also—and azure, and orange, and emerald. And the sinuous flickering of all seemed, not a pulsing of many waters, but a laboring of many wills—a fleeting conscious and monstrous—a writhing and a swarming incalculable, as of dragon-life in some depth of Erebus.

And life indeed was making the sinister splendor of that spectacle—but life infinitesimal, and of ghostliest delicacy—life illimitable, yet ephemeral, flaming and fading in ceaseless alternation over the whole round of waters even to the sky-line, above which, in the vaster abyss, other countless lights were throbbing with other spectral colors.

Watching, I wondered and I dreamed. I thought of the Ultimate Ghost revealed in that scintillation tremendous of Night and Sea;—quickening above me, in systems aglow with awful fusion of the past dissolved, with vapor of the life again to be;—quickening also beneath me, in meteor-gushings and constellations and nebulosities of colder fire—till I found myself doubting whether the million ages of the sun-star could really signify, in the flux of perpetual dissolution, anything more than the momentary sparkle of one expiring noctiluca.

Even with the doubt, the vision changed. I saw no longer the sea of the ancient East, with its shudderings of fire, but that Flood whose width and depth and altitude are one with the Night of Eternity—the shoreless and timeless Sea of Death and Birth. And the luminous haze of a hundred millions of suns—the Arch of the Milky Way—was a single smouldering surge in the flow of the Infinite Tides.

Yet again there came a change. I saw no more that vapory surge of suns; but the living darkness streamed and thrilled about me with infinite sparkling; and every sparkle was beating like a heart—beating out colors like the tints of the sea-fires. And the lampings of all continually flowed away, as shivering threads of radiance, into illimitable Mystery....

Then I knew myself also a phosphor-point—one fugitive floating sparkle of the measureless current;—and I saw that the light which was mine shifted tint with each changing of thought. Ruby it sometimes shone, and sometimes sapphire: now it was flame of topaz; again, it was fire of emerald. And the meaning of the changes I could not fully know. But thoughts of the earthly life seemed to make the light burn red; while thoughts of supernal being—of ghostly beauty and of ghostly bliss—seemed to kindle ineffable rhythms of azure and of violet.

But of white lights there were none in all the Visible. And I marveled.

Then a Voice said to me:—

"The White are of the Altitudes. By the blending of the billions they are made. Thy part is to help to their kindling. Even as the color of thy burning, so is the worth of thee. For a moment only is thy quickening; yet the light of thy pulsing lives on: by thy thought, in that shining moment, thou becomest a Maker of Gods."

RIKI-BAKA

His name was Riki, signifying Strength; but the people called him Riki-the-Simple, or Riki-the-Fool—"Riki-Baka,"—because he had been born into perpetual childhood. For the same reason they were kind to him—even when he set a house on fire by putting a lighted match to a mosquito-curtain, and clapped his hands for joy to see the blaze. At sixteen years he was a tall, strong lad; but in mind he remained always at the happy age of two, and therefore continued to play with very small children. The bigger children of the neighborhood, from four to seven years old, did not care to play with him, because he could not learn their songs and games. His favorite toy was a broomstick, which he used as a hobby-horse; and for hours at a time he would ride on that broomstick, up and down the slope in front of my house, with amazing peals of laughter. But at last he became troublesome by reason of his noise; and I had to tell him that he must find another playground. He bowed submissively, and then went off—sorrowfully trailing his broomstick behind him. Gentle at all times, and perfectly harmless if allowed no chance to play with fire, he seldom gave anybody cause for complaint. His relation to the life of our street was scarcely more than that of a dog or a chicken; and when he finally disappeared, I did not miss him. Months and months passed by before anything happened to remind me of Riki.

"What has become of Riki?" I then asked the old woodcutter who supplies our neighborhood with fuel. I remembered that Riki had often helped him to carry his bundles.

"Riki-Baka?" answered the old man. "Ah, Riki is dead—poor fellow!...Yes, he died nearly a year ago, very suddenly; the doctors said that he had some disease of the brain. And there is a strange story now about that poor Riki.

"When Riki died, his mother wrote his name, 'Riki-Baka,' in the palm of his left hand—putting 'Riki' in the Chinese character, and 'Baka' in *kana*.[88] And she repeated many prayers for him—prayers that he might be reborn into some more happy condition.

"Now, about three months ago, in the honorable residence of Nanigashi-Sama,[89] in Kojimachi,[90] a boy was born with characters on the palm of his left hand; and the characters were quite plain to read—'riki-baka!'

"So the people of that house knew that the birth must have happened in answer to somebody's prayer; and they caused inquiry to be made everywhere. At last a vegetable-seller brought word to them that there used to be a simple lad, called Riki-Baka, living in the Ushigome quarter, and that he had died during the last autumn; and they sent two men-servants to look for the mother of Riki.

"Those servants found the mother of Riki, and told her what had happened; and she was glad exceedingly—for that Nanigashi house is a very rich and famous house. But the servants said that the family of Nanigashi-Sama were very angry about the word 'Baka' on the child's hand. 'And where is your Riki buried?' the servants asked. 'He is buried in the cemetery of Zendoji,' she told them. 'Please to give us some of the clay of his grave,' they requested.

"So she went with them to the temple Zendoji, and showed them Riki's grave; and they took some of the grave-clay away with them, wrapped up in a *furoshiki*[91]....They gave Riki's mother some money—ten yen."...[92]

"But what did they want with that clay?" I inquired.

"Well," the old man answered, "you know that it would not do to let the child grow up with that name on his hand. And there is no other means of removing characters that come in

88   *Kana*: the Japanese phonetic alphabet.

89   "So-and-so": appellation used by Hearn in place of the real name.

90   A section of Tōkyō.

91   A square piece of cotton-goods, or other woven material, used as a wrapper in which to carry small packages.

92   Ten yen is nothing now, but was a formidable sum then.

that way upon the body of a child: *you must rub the skin with clay taken from the grave of the body of the former birth.*"...

NIGHTMARE-TOUCH

I

What *is* the fear of ghosts among those who believe in ghosts? All fear is the result of experience—experience of the individual or of the race—experience either of the present life or of lives forgotten. Even the fear of the unknown can have no other origin. And the fear of ghosts must be a product of past pain.

Probably the fear of ghosts, as well as the belief in them, had its beginning in dreams. It is a peculiar fear. No other fear is so intense; yet none is so vague. Feelings thus voluminous and dim are super-individual mostly—feelings inherited—feelings made within us by the experience of the dead.

What experience?

Nowhere do I remember reading a plain statement of the reason why ghosts are feared. Ask any ten intelligent persons of your acquaintance, who remember having once been afraid of ghosts, to tell you exactly why they were afraid—to define the fancy behind the fear;—and I doubt whether even one will be able to answer the question. The literature of folk-lore—oral and written—throws no clear light upon the subject. We find, indeed, various legends of men torn asunder by phantoms; but such gross imaginings could not explain the peculiar quality of ghostly fear. It is not a fear of bodily violence. It is not even a reasoning fear—not a fear that can readily explain itself—which would not be the case if it were founded upon definite ideas of physical danger. Furthermore, although primitive ghosts may have been imagined as capable of tearing and devouring, the common idea of a ghost is certainly that of a being intangible and imponderable.[93]

---

93   I may remark here that in many old Japanese legends and ballads, ghosts are represented as having power to *pull off* people's heads. But

Now I venture to state boldly that the common fear of ghosts is *the fear of being touched by ghosts*—or, in other words, that the imagined Supernatural is dreaded mainly because of its imagined power to touch. Only to *touch*, remember!—not to wound or to kill.

But this dread of the touch would itself be the result of experience—chiefly, I think, of prenatal experience stored up in the individual by inheritance, like the child's fear of darkness. And who can ever have had the sensation of being touched by ghosts? The answer is simple:—*Everybody who has been seized by phantoms in a dream.*

Elements of primeval fears—fears older than humanity—doubtless enter into the child-terror of darkness. But the more definite fear of ghosts may very possibly be composed with inherited results of dream-pain—ancestral experience of nightmare. And the intuitive terror of supernatural touch can thus be evolutionally explained.

Let me now try to illustrate my theory by relating some typical experiences.

II

When about five years old I was condemned to sleep by myself in a certain isolated room, thereafter always called the Child's Room. (At that time I was scarcely ever mentioned by name, but only referred to as "the Child.") The room was narrow, but very high, and, in spite of one tall window, very gloomy. It contained a fire-place wherein no fire was ever kindled; and the Child suspected that the chimney was haunted.

A law was made that no light should be left in the Child's Room at night—simply because the Child was afraid of the dark. His fear of the dark was judged to be a mental disorder requiring

---

so far as the origin of the fear of ghosts is concerned, such stories explain nothing—since the experiences that evolved the fear must have been real, not imaginary, experiences.

severe treatment. But the treatment aggravated the disorder. Previously I had been accustomed to sleep in a well-lighted room, with a nurse to take care of me. I thought that I should die of fright when sentenced to lie alone in the dark, and—what seemed to me then abominably cruel—actually *locked* into my room, the most dismal room of the house. Night after night when I had been warmly tucked into bed, the lamp was removed; the key clicked in the lock; the protecting light and the footsteps of my guardian receded together. Then an agony of fear would come upon me. Something in the black air would seem to gather and grow—(I thought that I could even *hear* it grow)—till I had to scream. Screaming regularly brought punishment; but it also brought back the light, which more than consoled for the punishment. This fact being at last found out, orders were given to pay no further heed to the screams of the Child.

Why was I thus insanely afraid? Partly because the dark had always been peopled for me with shapes of terror. So far back as memory extended, I had suffered from ugly dreams; and when aroused from them I could always *see* the forms dreamed of, lurking in the shadows of the room. They would soon fade out; but for several moments they would appear like tangible realities. And they were always the same figures.... Sometimes, without any preface of dreams, I used to see them at twilight-time— following me about from room to room, or reaching long dim hands after me, from story to story, up through the interspaces of the deep stairways.

I had complained of these haunters only to be told that I must never speak of them, and that they did not exist. I had complained to everybody in the house; and everybody in the house had told me the very same thing. But there was the evidence of my eyes! The denial of that evidence I could explain only in two ways:—Either the shapes were afraid of big people, and showed themselves to me alone, because I was little and weak; or else the entire household had agreed, for some ghastly reason, to say what was not true. This latter theory seemed to me the more probable one, because I had several times perceived the shapes when I was not unattended;—and the consequent appearance of secrecy frightened me scarcely less than the visions did. Why was I forbidden to talk about what I saw, and even heard—on creaking stairways—behind wavering curtains?

"Nothing will hurt you,"—this was the merciless answer to all my pleadings not to be left alone at night. But the haunters *did* hurt me. Only—they would wait until after I had fallen asleep, and so into their power—for they possessed occult means of preventing me from rising or moving or crying out.

Needless to comment upon the policy of locking me up alone with these fears in a black room. Unutterably was I tormented in that room—for years! Therefore I felt relatively happy when sent away at last to a children's boarding-school, where the haunters very seldom ventured to show themselves.

They were not like any people that I had ever known. They were shadowy dark-robed figures, capable of atrocious self-distortion—capable, for instance, of growing up to the ceiling, and then across it, and then lengthening themselves, head-down-wards, along the opposite wall. Only their faces were distinct; and I tried not to look at their faces. I tried also in my dreams— or thought that I tried—to awaken myself from the sight of them by pulling at my eyelids with my fingers; but the eyelids would remain closed, as if sealed.... Many years afterwards, the frightful plates in Orfila's *Traité des Exhumés*, beheld for the first time, recalled to me with a sickening start the dream-terrors of child-hood. But to understand the Child's experience, you must imagine Orfila's drawings intensely alive, and continually elongating or distorting, as in some monstrous anamorphosis.

Nevertheless the mere sight of those nightmare-faces was not the worst of the experiences in the Child's Room. The dreams always began with a suspicion, or sensation of something heavy in the air—slowly quenching will—slowly numbing my power to move. At such times I usually found myself alone in a large unlighted apartment; and, almost simultaneously with the first sensation of fear, the atmosphere of the room would become suffused, half-way to the ceiling, with a sombre-yellowish glow, making objects dimly visible—though the ceiling itself remained pitch-black. This was not a true appearance of light: rather it seemed as if the black air were changing color from beneath.... Certain terrible aspects of sunset, on the eve of storm, offer like effects of sinister color.... Forthwith I would try to escape— (feeling at every step a sensation *as of wading*)—and would sometimes succeed in struggling half-way across the room;—but there I would always find myself brought to a standstill—paralyzed by some innominable opposition. Happy voices I could hear in the next room;—I could see light through the transom over the door that I had vainly endeavored to reach;—I knew that one loud cry would save me. But not even by the most frantic effort could I raise my voice above a whisper.... And all this signified only that the Nameless was coming—was nearing— was mounting the stairs. I could hear the step—booming like the sound of a muffled drum—and I wondered why nobody else heard it. A long, long time the haunter would take to come— malevolently pausing after each ghastly footfall. Then, without a creak, the bolted door would open—slowly, slowly—and the thing would enter, gibbering soundlessly—and put out hands— and clutch me—and toss me to the black ceiling—and catch me descending to toss me up again, and again, and again.... In those moments the feeling was not fear: fear itself had been torpified by the first seizure. It was a sensation that has no name in the language of the living. For every touch brought a shock of something infinitely worse than pain—something that thrilled into the innermost secret being of me—a sort of abominable electricity, discovering unimagined capacities of suffering in totally unfamiliar regions of sentiency.... This was commonly the work of a single tormentor; but I can also remember having been caught by a group, and tossed from one to another—seemingly for a time of many minutes.

III

Whence the fancy of those shapes? I do not know. Possibly from some impression of fear in earliest infancy; possibly from some experience of fear in other lives than mine. That mystery is forever insoluble. But the mystery of the shock of the touch admits of a definite hypothesis.

First, allow me to observe that the experience of the sensation itself cannot be dismissed as "mere imagination." Imagination means cerebral activity: its pains and its pleasures are alike inseparable from nervous operation, and their physical importance is sufficiently proved by their physiological effects. Dream-fear may kill as well as other fear; and no emotion thus powerful can be reasonably deemed undeserving of study.

One remarkable fact in the problem to be considered is that the sensation of seizure in dreams differs totally from all sensations familiar to ordinary waking life. Why this differentiation? How interpret the extraordinary massiveness and depth of the thrill?

I have already suggested that the dreamer's fear is most probably not a reflection of relative experience, but represents the incalculable total of ancestral experience of dream-fear. If the sum of the experience of active life be transmitted by inheritance, so must likewise be transmitted the summed experience of the life of sleep. And in normal heredity either class of transmissions would probably remain distinct.

Now, granting this hypothesis, the sensation of dream-seizure would have had its beginnings in the earliest phases of dream-consciousness—long prior to the apparition of man. The first creatures capable of thought and fear must often have dreamed of being caught by their natural enemies. There could not have been much imagining of pain in these primal dreams. But higher nervous development in later forms of being would have been accompanied with larger susceptibility to dream-pain. Still later, with the growth of reasoning-power, ideas of the supernatural would have changed and intensified the character of dream-fear. Furthermore, through all the course of evolution, heredity would have been accumulating the experience of such feeling. Under those forms of imaginative pain evolved through reaction of religious beliefs, there would persist some dim survival of savage primitive fears, and again, under this, a dimmer but incomparably deeper substratum of ancient animal-terrors. In the dreams of the modern child all these latencies might quicken— one below another—unfathomably—with the coming and the growing of nightmare.

It may be doubted whether the phantasms of any particular nightmare have a history older than the brain in which they move. But the shock of the touch would seem to indicate *some point of dream-contact with the total race-experience of shadowy seizure*. It may be that profundities of Self—abysses never reached by any ray from the life of sun—are strangely stirred in slumber, and that out of their blackness immediately responds a shuddering of memory, measureless even by millions of years.

HI-MAWARI

On the wooded hill behind the house Robert and I are looking for fairy-rings. Robert is eight years old, comely, and very wise;—I am a little more than seven—and I reverence Robert. It is a glowing glorious August day; and the warm air is filled with sharp sweet scents of resin.

We do not find any fairy-rings; but we find a great many pine-cones in the high grass... I tell Robert the old Welsh story of the man who went to sleep, unawares, inside a fairy-ring, and so disappeared for seven years, and would never eat or speak after his friends had delivered him from the enchantment.

"They eat nothing but the points of needles, you know," says Robert.

"Who?" I ask.

"Goblins," Robert answers.

This revelation leaves me dumb with astonishment and awe... But Robert suddenly cries out:—

"There is a Harper!—he is coming to the house!"

And down the hill we run to hear the harper... But what a harper! Not like the hoary minstrels of the picture-books. A swarthy, sturdy, unkempt vagabond, with black bold eyes under scowling black brows. More like a bricklayer than a bard—and his garments are corduroy!

"Wonder if he is going to sing in Welsh?" murmurs Robert.

I feel too much disappointed to make any remarks. The harper poses his harp—a huge instrument—upon our door-step, sets all the strings ringing with a sweep of his grimy fingers, clears his throat with a sort of angry growl, and begins—

> *Believe me, if all those endearing young charms,*
> *Which I gaze on so fondly to-day...*

The accent, the attitude, the voice, all fill me with repulsion unutterable—shock me with a new sensation of formidable vulgarity. I want to cry out loud, "You have no right to sing that song!" For I have heard it sung by the lips of the dearest and fairest being in my little world;—and that this rude, coarse man should dare to sing it vexes me like a mockery—angers me like an insolence. But only for a moment!... With the utterance of the syllables "to-day," that deep, grim voice suddenly breaks into a quivering tenderness indescribable;—then, marvelously changing, it mellows into tones sonorous and rich as the bass of a great organ—while a sensation unlike anything ever felt before takes me by the throat... What witchcraft has he learned? What secret has he found—this scowling man of the road?... Oh! Is there anybody else in the whole world who can sing like that?... And the form of the singer flickers and dims;—and the house, and the lawn, and all visible shapes of things tremble and swim before me. Yet instinctively I fear that man;—I almost hate him; and I feel myself flushing with anger and shame because of his power to move me thus...

"He made you cry," Robert compassionately observes, to my further confusion—as the harper strides away, richer by a gift of sixpence taken without thanks... "But I think he must be a gipsy. Gipsies are bad people—and they are wizards... Let us go back to the wood."

We climb again to the pines, and there squat down upon the sun-flecked grass, and look over town and sea. But we do not play as before: the spell of the wizard is strong upon us both... "Perhaps he is a goblin," I venture at last, "or a fairy?" "No," says Robert—"only a gipsy. But that is nearly as bad. They steal children, you know."...

"What shall we do if he comes up here?" I gasp, in sudden terror at the lonesomeness of our situation.

"Oh, he wouldn't dare," answers Robert—"not by daylight, you know."...

[Only yesterday, near the village of Takata, I noticed a flower which the Japanese call by nearly the same name as we do: Himawari, "The Sunward-turning;"—and over the space of forty years there thrilled back to me the voice of that wandering harper—

As the Sunflower turns on her god, when he sets,
The same look that she turned when he rose.

Again I saw the sun-flecked shadows on that far Welsh hill; and Robert for a moment again stood beside me, with his girl's face and his curls of gold. We were looking for fairy-rings... But all that existed of the real Robert must long ago have suffered a sea-change into something rich and strange... Greater love hath no man than this, that a man lay down his life for his friend...]

HORAI

Blue vision of depth lost in height—sea and sky interblending through luminous haze. The day is of spring, and the hour morning.

Only sky and sea—one azure enormity... In the fore, ripples are catching a silvery light, and threads of foam are swirling. But a little further off no motion is visible, nor anything save color: dim warm blue of water widening away to melt into blue of air. Horizon there is none: only distance soaring into space—infinite concavity hollowing before you, and hugely arching above you— the color deepening with the height. But far in the midway-blue there hangs a faint, faint vision of palace towers, with high roofs horned and curved like moons—some shadowing of splendor strange and old, illumined by a sunshine soft as memory.

...What I have thus been trying to describe is a *kakemono*— that is to say, a Japanese painting on silk, suspended to the wall of my alcove;—and the name of it is *Shinkiro*, which signifies "Mirage." But the shapes of the mirage are unmistakable. Those are the glimmering portals of Horai the blest; and those are the moony roofs of the Palace of the Dragon-King;—and the fashion of them (though limned by a Japanese brush of to-day) is the fashion of things Chinese, twenty-one hundred years ago...

Thus much is told of the place in the Chinese books of that time:—

In Horai there is neither death nor pain; and there is no winter. The flowers in that place never fade, and the fruits never fail; and if a man taste of those fruits even but once, he can never again feel thirst or hunger. In Horai grow the enchanted plants *So-rin-shi*, and *Riku-go-aoi*, and *Ban-kon-to*, which heal all manner of sickness;—and there grows also the magical grass *Yo-shin-shi*, that quickens the dead; and the magical grass is watered by a fairy water of which a single drink confers perpetual youth. The people of Horai eat their rice out of very, very small bowls; but the rice never diminishes within those bowls—however much of it be eaten—until the eater desires no more. And the people of Horai drink their wine out of very, very small cups; but no man can empty one of those cups—however stoutly he may drink—until there comes upon him the pleasant drowsiness of intoxication.

All this and more is told in the legends of the time of the Shin Dynasty. But that the people who wrote down those legends ever saw Horai, even in a mirage, is not believable. For really there are no enchanted fruits which leave the eater forever satisfied—nor any magical grass which revives the dead—nor any fountain of fairy water—nor any bowls which never lack rice—nor any cups which never lack wine. It is not true that sorrow and death never enter Horai;—neither is it true that there is not any winter. The winter in Horai is cold;—and winds then bite to the bone; and the heaping of snow is monstrous on the roofs of the Dragon-King.

Nevertheless there are wonderful things in Horai; and the most wonderful of all has not been mentioned by any Chinese writer. I mean the atmosphere of Horai. It is an atmosphere peculiar to the place; and, because of it, the sunshine in Horai is *whiter* than any other sunshine—a milky light that never dazzles—astonishingly clear, but very soft. This atmosphere is not of our human period: it is enormously old—so old that I feel afraid when I try to think how old it is;—and it is not a mixture of nitrogen and oxygen. It is not made of air at all, but of ghost—the substance of quintillions of quintillions of generations of souls blended into one immense translucency—souls of people who thought in ways never resembling our ways. Whatever mortal man inhales that atmosphere, he takes into his blood the thrilling of these spirits; and they change the sense within him—reshaping his notions of Space and Time—so that he can see only as they used to see, and feel only as they used to feel, and think only as they used to think. Soft as sleep are these changes of sense; and Horai, discerned across them, might thus be described:—

—Because in Horai there is no knowledge of great evil, the hearts of the people never grow old. And, by reason of being always young in heart, the people of Horai smile from birth until death—except when the Gods send sorrow among them; and faces then are veiled until the sorrow goes away. All folk in Horai love and trust each other, as if all were members of a single household;—and the speech of the women is like birdsong, because the hearts of them are light as the souls of birds;—and the swaying of the sleeves of the maidens at play seems a flutter of wide, soft wings. In Horai nothing is hidden but grief, because there is no reason for shame;—and nothing is locked away, because there could not be any theft;—and by night as well as by day all doors remain unbarred, because there is no reason for fear. And because the people are fairies— though mortal—all things in Horai, except the Palace of the Dragon-King, are small and quaint and queer;—and these fairy-folk do really eat their rice out of very, very small bowls, and drink their wine out of very, very small cups...

—Much of this seeming would be due to the inhalation of that ghostly atmosphere—but not all. For the spell wrought by the dead is only the charm of an Ideal, the glamor of an ancient hope;—and something of that hope has found fulfilment in many hearts—in the simple beauty of unselfish lives—in the sweetness of Woman...

—Evil winds from the West are blowing over Horai; and the magical atmosphere, alas! Is shrinking away before them. It lingers now in patches only, and bands—like those long bright bands of cloud that train across the landscapes of Japanese painters. Under these shreds of the elfish vapor you still can find Horai— but not everywhere... Remember that Horai is also called *Shinkiro*, which signifies Mirage—the Vision of the Intangible. And the Vision is fading—never again to appear save in pictures and poems and dreams...

JIU-ROKU-ZAKURA

In Wakegori, a district of the province of Iyō, there is a very ancient and famous cherry-tree, called *Jiu-roku-zakura*, or "the Cherry-tree of the Sixteenth Day," because it blooms every year upon the sixteenth day of the first month (by the old lunar calendar)—and only upon that day. Thus the time of its flowering is the Period of Great Cold—though the natural habit of a cherry-tree is to wait for the spring season before venturing to blossom. But the *Jiu-roku-zakura* blossoms with a life that is not—or, at least, that was not originally—its own. There is the ghost of a man in that tree.

He was a samurai of Iyō; and the tree grew in his garden; and it used to flower at the usual time—that is to say, about the end of March or the beginning of April. He had played under that tree when he was a child; and his parents and grandparents and ancestors had hung to its blossoming branches, season after season for more than a hundred years, bright strips of colored paper inscribed with poems of praise. He himself became very old—outliving all his children; and there was nothing in the world left for him to love except that tree. And lo! In the summer of a certain year, the tree withered and died!

Exceedingly the old man sorrowed for his tree. Then kind neighbors found for him a young and beautiful cherry-tree, and planted it in his garden—hoping thus to comfort him. And he thanked them, and pretended to be glad. But really his heart was full of pain; for he had loved the old tree so well that nothing could have consoled him for the loss of it.

At last there came to him a happy thought: he remembered a way by which the perishing tree might be saved. (It was the sixteenth day of the first month.) Along he went into his garden, and bowed down before the withered tree, and spoke to it, saying:"Now deign, I beseech you, once more to bloom—because I am going to die in your stead." (For it is believed that one can really give away one's life to another person, or to a creature or even to a tree, by the favor of the gods;—and thus to transfer one's life is expressed by the term *migawari ni tatsu*, "to act as a substitute.") Then under that tree he spread a white cloth, and divers coverings, and sat down upon the coverings, and performed *hara-kiri* after the fashion of a samurai. And the ghost of him went into the tree, and made it blossom in that same hour.

And every year it still blooms on the sixteenth day of the first month, in the season of snow.